*To R.Z., somewhere between
married and Buenos Aires.*

NO ESCAPE

Norah McClintock

Photography by
Rodrigo Moreno

Cover design by
Andrea Casault

SCHOLASTIC CANADA LTD.

Toronto New York London Auckland Sydney
Mexico City New Delhi Hong Kong Buenos Aires

Scholastic Canada Ltd.
175 Hillmount Road, Markham, Ontario L6C 1Z7, Canada

Scholastic Inc.
555 Broadway, New York, NY 10012, USA

Scholastic Australia Pty Limited
PO Box 579, Gosford, NSW 2250, Australia

Scholastic New Zealand Limited
Private Bag 94407, Greenmount, Auckland, New Zealand

Scholastic Ltd.
Villiers House, Clarendon Avenue, Leamington Spa,
Warwickshire CV32 5PR, UK

National Library of Canada Cataloguing in Publication

McClintock, Norah
  No escape / Norah McClintock.

ISBN 0-439-96905-0

I. Title.

PS8575.C62N6 2003   jC813'.54   C2003-901061-9
PZ7

6 5 4 3 2 1   Printed in Canada   03 04 05 06 07

CHAPTER ONE

I've never heard of a school that doesn't have at least one Kyle Darke.

You know, the guy who's older than everyone else in any of his classes because he never makes the grade, grade-wise. Kyle was seventeen. Technically, he didn't even have to be in school anymore. Most people I knew were surprised that he hadn't just emptied his locker and called it an academic day. The only subject he did well in was French — don't ask me why. I'd heard that he was a year or two behind in everything else. Even if he decided all of a sudden to apply himself, he'd probably be celebrating his twenty-first birthday by the time he got enough credits to graduate. No one I knew thought Kyle was the kind of guy who could pull off that sort of minor miracle.

He was tall — he'd have been a natural on a basketball court, but he wasn't the kind of guy you associated with teamwork — and had long, skinny arms and longer, skinnier legs. His thick black hair hung over his shoulders and flopped into his eyes. He always walked sort of hunched over — maybe so he'd look smaller and less conspicuous, but it didn't work. You always noticed Kyle, even though he was usually in the background, usually looking at the floor, never saying much of anything, except, apparently, in French. I knew that because he was in my kid sister Phoebe's class. He sat — where else? — at the very back of the room.

Phoebe said that when Madame Benoit called on him, he always answered. She told me that he talked in such a soft voice that Madame Benoit had to come halfway down the aisle to catch what he was saying, but that when he had finished, she always smiled and said things like, "*Très bien*, Kyle" or "*Merveilleux*, Kyle" or "*Parfait*, Kyle." Go figure.

And now, I was about to press my lips to Kyle Darke's face.

* * *

It had started with one too many Friday-morning whacks on the snooze alarm and an assumption — which had turned out to be faulty — that if I didn't appear downstairs on time, someone would yell a warning to me. Okay, so I hit the snooze alarm a couple of extra times because I had stayed up much later than I should have. But I had been reading, and reading is good, right? Even if what you're reading wouldn't make your average high-school English teacher jump for joy.

I guess it also wouldn't have hurt to remember that Mr. Mowat had planned something "special" for us that day. Mr. Mowat taught phys. ed., and was subbing as my homeroom teacher while my regular homeroom teacher was on maternity leave. He'd been organizing basic first-aid classes for the school throughout the year and these had finally worked their way around to me. That's why I had reported to the gym instead of my homeroom class-room.

It was also why everyone in the gym was already sitting in pairs. Well, almost everyone. The only one sitting alone — the only one who hadn't looked up when I made my entry — was Kyle Darke.

As I looked for a place to sit, Mr. Mowat said, "So glad you could make it, Chloe." Mr. Mowat was the kind of guy who routinely told his starting line, "Any of you guys brings an excuse why you didn't make practice on time, it better be a death certifi-cate."

"Oh, good," the woman instructor said. "Now we have no odd men out. Please join your partner." She waved her hand toward Kyle while the gym echoed with laughter — and snickering.

There was a time in my life when I would have walked out of a class rather than pair up with someone like Kyle. This wasn't that time. *You are a mature person,* I told myself. *You can handle this. You can handle anything.*

"Now," the first-aid woman said, "you have each been given an envelope containing a disposable mask. You may open those envelopes now and care-fully remove the masks."

"Masks?" I said. I glanced over at Sarah Moran, who was in the same homeroom as me.

She smiled sweetly at me. "We're doing mouth-to-mouth artificial respiration," she said.

But of course.

* * *

It could have been worse. I could have been stuck with a wannabe player like Rick Antonio. You know, the kind of guy who salivates at the thought of doing mouth-to-mouth with a girl. I glanced across the gym and saw him grinning at me. He had paired himself with his current girlfriend, Kim Timberly (what had her parents been thinking?). They had staked out the farthest corner of the gym.

We listened to the first-aid lady's instructions. We watched her demonstrate the technique on Mr. Mowat — plenty of giggles all around at that. Then it was time for us to practise.

I turned to Kyle, who was still staring resolutely at the floor. It made me wonder why he had even bothered to show up.

"You want to go first or you want me to go first?" I said. Both options were triggering my gag reflex.

Kyle said nothing.

Okay, then. "Lie down, Kyle," I said. To be honest, I expected resistance. Or maybe some smart-ass answer. I got neither. Instead, Kyle unfolded his long, skinny body onto the floor.

"Okay, remember: step by step, people," the first-aid lady said. "And don't forget any steps. When you're in an emergency, you want to have this information imprinted on your brain."

I glanced around and saw twenty-nine would-be respirators saying to their fake-unconscious partners, "Are you okay?" while they gently tapped their victims' shoulders. I did the same to Kyle. Then we all turned to our own personal Mr. Invisible Bystander and said, "Get medical help. Call 911." We were obviously not playing with a worst-case scenario here.

Then came the fun part. I had to touch Kyle Darke.

We didn't actually have to breathe into our partners' mouths — and we had those disposable masks as barriers between their skin and ours — but I still had to tilt Kyle's head back and lift his jaw to open his airway. And I had to keep my hand on his forehead to make sure his head didn't slip back. Eeew!

I followed each step. I didn't skip any. But mostly what imprinted itself on my brain was, *Never hit that snooze button again. Ever!*

Then it was my turn to pretend I was out cold, and Kyle's turn to attempt to resuscitate me. I lay down on my back and closed my eyes. I'm not sure what I expected. Maybe that he wouldn't even try to do it. Or that he'd get it all wrong. What actually happened was that I heard Kyle say, in a barely audible voice, "Are you okay?" I heard him instruct Mr. Nobody to go for help. I felt his warm, dry hands gently tip my head back. Then a mask was placed over my mouth and Kyle Darke went through his routine without any hesitation. Go figure.

* * *

For the rest of the day, no matter where I went and who I ran into, I got razzed about doing mouth-to-mouth with Kyle Darke.

"New boyfriend, Chloe?"

Yeah, right.

"Prom date, Chloe?"

Ha, ha.

And, from Rick Antonio, "Tongue, Chloe?"

"That's not the part of the anatomy that springs to mind when I think of you, Rick," I said.

It was a relief to hear the last bell of the day.

* * *

Usually I leave school on Friday afternoons with the words of Martin Luther King echoing in my head: *Free at last, free at last.* Usually that sentiment carries me all the way home. But usually my kid sister isn't standing at the front entrance of the school, ready to kill my euphoria.

Phoebe was leaning against the railing that ran along one side of the school parking lot. She's only sixteen months younger than me, and about the same height, but her hair is blond, her eyes are blue and her skin is creamy white tinged with pink. We have the same mother, but not the same father. Don't ask.

She started up the steps toward me as soon as she saw me.

"What?" I said, automatically and not one hundred percent nicely. I admit it, I'm not every little sister's dream sibling. But then Phoebe has a habit of beginning most conversations with, "Can I borrow . . . " That is, when she bothers to ask.

Phoebe backed down two steps and was about to back down a few more when my kinder, gentler side kicked in. "Keep that up and you're going to fall," I said.

She spun around and descended the rest of the steps in the Mom-approved way, face forward. She didn't say a word.

"So, what do you want?" I asked finally.

She peeked sideways at me, studying me and biting the inside of her lip.

"There's this guy," she began slowly. Then she shook her head. "Never mind."

We walked side by side out of the schoolyard and up toward Centre Street, the main street in the town of East Hastings where we had lived for — I could hardly believe it! — almost an entire year. I knew Phoebe hadn't been waiting for me after school just to tell me "never mind." But if she thought I was going to play games with her — *Come on, Phoebe, you can tell me;* please *tell me* — well, she could think again.

The route we were walking took us past the police station. Usually it's pretty quiet around there, but today something was going on. Three men stood on the sidewalk in front of the station house. One of them was yelling at East Hastings's chief of police, who just happens to be my stepfather, Louis Levesque.

Phoebe tugged on my arm to drag me to a halt. She needn't have bothered. I had already stopped to see what was going on.

"Your job is to protect the citizens of this town," the man was saying. His face was crimson with rage. The two other men stood on either side of him. I recognized one of them, Charles Tyson, manager of the Canadian Tire store where my mother works. He looked just as angry as the man who was doing all the yelling.

Levesque was standing on the first step leading up to the main door of the police station. Steve Denby, another of East Hastings's finest, stood just behind him.

Levesque listened to what was being said. He looked at each of the three men in turn. "My job is to protect *all* the citizens of this town," he said, "and to see that no one breaks the law. If they do, then it's my job to arrest them." He said all this quietly. He always spoke quietly and always stayed calm, which usually gave him the advantage in a tense situation. But he always stood a certain way, too, with his hands up near his belt. It had taken me a while to figure that one out, but now I knew. He was ready — he was always ready — in case he had to draw his gun, which, so far, I had never seen him do.

"That man forfeited citizenship in this town nine years ago," the angry man said.

"Who is that guy?" I said to Phoebe.

"That's Daniel Tyson," a voice beside me said.

I turned. It was Eric Moore, sports editor of the *East Hastings Herald*, the school newspaper. I had been press-ganged by my English teacher into working as a reporter on the paper. No one had had to twist Eric's arm, though. He was the rarest of jocks — a sports fanatic who could write circles around the average English-literature whiz kid.

"And that guy on his right is Jimmy Johnston," Eric said. "He runs that big hunting and fishing camp east of the park."

I'd heard of the camp. It was hugely popular with American businessmen who felt an annual urge to shoot something defenceless. I never could see the sport in hunting — guys with high-tech guns versus unarmed Bambis. These were the same kind of guys who went fishing with sonar and considered themselves geniuses of the high seas when they managed to catch something.

"No one has forfeited any rights," Levesque said. "East Hastings is his home as much as it is yours. And I'm going to expect you to respect that and to let the man live in peace."

Daniel Tyson glowered at Levesque. "We'll see," he said. "We'll just see how many people agree with you." He turned and nodded to his companions. The three of them stalked away.

Levesque started to turn to go back inside. He spotted me and shook his head slowly. I knew what that meant: *Not now, Chloe.*

"I wonder what that was all about," I said. "Who were they talking about, anyway?"

"Caleb," Eric said. "They were talking about Caleb Darke."

Phoebe made a noise that sounded like a gasp. When I glanced over at her, she was staring down at the pavement.

CHAPTER TWO

"Caleb Darke, as in Kyle Darke?" I said.

Eric nodded. "His brother."

"What about him?"

"His sentence is up," Eric said. "He'll be back in town tomorrow."

"Sentence?" I said. "Kyle's brother was in prison?" Nobody had mentioned that to me. I wondered if Phoebe knew. I glanced at her again. She looked as surprised as I was.

"He got eight years for what he supposedly did," Eric said.

Interesting choice of words. "Supposedly?" I said.

"He was convicted of aggravated assault," Eric said.

Kyle's brother had been in prison for aggravated assault and I'd never heard about it? "He got *eight* years?" I said. "For assault?"

"Aggravated assault," Eric said.

"But eight years? I'm no expert," I said — and I'm not; I just happen to live in the same house as a cop, which has made me aware of things I never used to think about — "but I'm pretty sure I've heard of people serving less time for more serious crimes."

"You probably have," Eric said. "Most people do a year and a half, maybe two years, for aggravated assault. The maximum sentence is fourteen years.

But the Crown asked for a sentence of ten to twelve years for Caleb, because the person he supposedly assaulted ended up in a coma. For a long time, nobody thought she was going to live. At best, they thought she'd end up a vegetable."

"She?" I said. "Who did he assault — I mean, *supposedly* assault?"

"His fiancée. Terri Tyson."

"As in Daniel and Charles Tyson?" I said.

Eric nodded. "Daniel Tyson is her father. Charles is her brother."

I remembered something Mom had told me back when she started work at the Canadian Tire, a month or so after we'd moved to East Hastings from Montreal. "Charles has a sister who's brain-damaged," I said.

"That's Terri. Somebody beat her up pretty badly." *Somebody*? Another interesting choice of words. "She eventually came out of her coma, but she never really recovered. It'll be nine years come September."

"And the somebody who was convicted was Kyle's brother?" I said. "Why would he do something like that?"

"Supposedly because Terri was breaking up with him."

There was that word again — supposedly.

"At least, that's what the Tysons said," Eric added. "Caleb denied it. And Terri wasn't able to say anything at all. The Tysons think Caleb should have been charged with attempted murder, but he wasn't. Instead, it was aggravated assault. He was convicted. He only got out on statutory release." He gave me a look that told me *this is a big deal*, but I didn't understand why. "For something like that, you're usually eligible for parole after you've done a third of your sentence," Eric said. "He got turned down. The parole board didn't like the fact that he refused to take responsibility for what he'd done. After you've served two-thirds of your sentence, they let you out on statutory release, but you're supervised for the rest of the time you would have served. He's been living down in Toronto. It was a condition of his release that he stay away from Terri. But now his eight years are up. He's coming back to East Hastings tomorrow."

"Eric, the way you're talking, it sounds like you think he's innocent," I said.

"Caleb says he is."

I glanced back at the police station and thought about the three angry faces I had just seen there. "Not everyone seems to agree."

Eric shrugged. "My uncle is a criminal lawyer. He defended Caleb. The only time I ever hated living in this town was during that trial. People used to call our house. They'd leave messages for my dad. 'Your brother is a traitor to his home town.' Stuff like that." He shook his head. "Looks like some people are never going to give Caleb a break, no matter how much time he served." He adjusted his backpack on his shoulder, shifting it with a slow, rolling movement, as if it weighed fifty kilos. "See

12

you," he said. He crossed the street and headed slowly away from us.

I looked at Phoebe. "Think we should go in?" I said. Go in to the police station, I meant, to see if we could worm some details out of Levesque.

Phoebe shook her head. "What's the point?" she said. "He won't tell you anything."

This is one of the big differences between Phoebe and me, at least the way Mom tells it. When Phoebe was a baby and Mom would tell her not to touch something — "No, Phoebe!" — Phoebe would freeze. Phoebe hates anyone to disapprove of her — well, anyone in authority. She doesn't seem to care what *I* think. But when I was little and Mom told me not to touch something — "No, Chloe!" — I'd turn right around and do exactly what I'd been told not to do and, Mom claims, I'd just dare her to punish me. Mom generally took that dare. My older sister, Brynn, who is at CEGEP in Montreal, would look at Mom, shrug and find something else to do. Something *constructive*, according to Mom.

I didn't barge into the police station, however. Instead, I walked home with Phoebe. In silence, as it turned out. Suddenly she didn't want to talk to me about whatever it was she'd been bursting to tell me after school, and I still wasn't about to beg her.

As for getting information out of Levesque — well, I told myself that it was all a matter of timing.

* * *

13

Levesque wasn't home for supper. It was just Mom and Phoebe and me. Letterman was over by the time Shendor lifted her head off my lap and rowfed. A moment later I heard a car door slam in the driveway. Then the front door opened.

"What are you doing up?" Levesque said from the entrance to the living room. He bent over and scratched Shendor behind her ears.

"It's Friday night," I said.

"Where's your mother?"

"In bed. Probably sound asleep."

He sighed before disappearing into the kitchen. I heard the fridge door open. I glanced back at the TV. A late-night talk show was on. The host was talking to a guy who had made a few bad movies back in the eighties. I hit the remote's *Off* button. When I got to the kitchen, Levesque was standing in front of the open fridge, staring into it. Finally he pulled out a jug of orange juice and poured himself a glass.

"What's going to happen about Caleb Darke?" I asked.

He looked only moderately surprised. "What do you know about that?"

"Just what I heard around," I said. "Sounds like some people don't want him here."

Levesque sighed as he put the jug of juice back into the fridge.

"Some people don't want a lot of things," he said.

"You expecting trouble tomorrow?"

No answer. Just a shrug.

"It's been a long day," he said. "And I have the feeling tomorrow is going to be another long one." He swallowed the rest of his juice, rinsed his glass, put it into the dishwasher and left the kitchen. I heard him climb the stairs quietly, so he wouldn't disturb Mom or Phoebe.

Okay, so timing wasn't everything.

* * *

I got up early for a Saturday. According to Eric, Caleb Darke was supposed to arrive on the ten o'clock bus. The intercity bus dropped off and picked up passengers just outside Benny's, a combination grocery store, pharmacy, hardware store and tourist trap. It sold maple-sugar candy shaped like maple leaves, beaded belts supposedly made by native people but really made in China, and T-shirts that read *Beautiful Downtown East Hastings*. It did a rip-roaring business between the end of May and Thanksgiving — cottage season — but was a whole lot quieter during the rest of the year.

Benny's is out on Centre Street, just before it branches off to the highway. It has a generous parking lot that seemed awfully crowded for nine-thirty on a Saturday morning in early May. The place was jammed with cars and people, some of them carrying signs that read, *East Hastings: A Peaceful Town* and *Keep Our Town Safe*. A lot of signs showed a cartoon of a guy in a prison uniform — you know, the striped shirt and pants and the ankle shackled to a ball and chain — with a big red circle around it and a red slash through the circle.

It added up to a lot of anti-Caleb sentiment.

I scanned the crowd and spotted Daniel and Charles Tyson, and Jimmy Johnston. Dozens of other people had turned out too. They were all clustered together — talking, drinking coffee out of paper cups and looking generally disgruntled. Two East Hastings patrol cars were parked at the edges of the crowd. Levesque was standing beside one of them, Steve Denby beside the other. Over on the far side of the parking lot, standing side by side, were Eric Moore and Kyle Darke. I headed for them.

Eric nodded at me. Kyle didn't even look up.

"You two know each other?" Eric said.

I nodded. "We did first-aid together yesterday."

Kyle raised his head slowly, looked at me and . . . what do you know? Surprise registered in his eyes.

"Chloe's a friend of mine," Eric said. "We work on the school paper together."

Kyle studied me for a few moments, then turned to look at the growing crowd.

"You sure your dad is going to be able to handle this?" Eric said.

Kyle's head swivelled around to look at me again. "Dad?" he said.

"He's the chief of police," Eric said. He nodded to where Levesque was standing.

Kyle stared at me, then looked back at Levesque.

"You don't look like him," he said.

A rather elementary observation, my dear Watson. My real father was Chinese, which explains why I'm the only person in my family with long, straight black hair and dark almond-shaped eyes. I've had more than my share of people asking me where I'm from. For the record, I was born and raised in Montreal.

"He's my step-father," I told Kyle.

"He's a cop."

I hated people jumping to all kinds of conclusions about me, just because Mom had decided to marry a cop. Like it had anything to do with me. Like I'd had any choice in the matter.

"Yeah?" I said. "So?" When I'm angry, I'm *supremely* angry. The kind of force you don't want to be in the path of — or so I've been told.

Kyle shifted his eyes back to the ground. Eric nudged me with his elbow. I ignored him and glanced at my watch.

By a quarter to ten, it looked like half of East Hastings was jammed into Benny's parking lot. Even Phoebe had shown up. I spotted her out near the road. At ten minutes to ten, three OPP squad cars pulled up. Six officers got out. Three of them stayed with the cars. The other three went over to Levesque. I watched them confer, and then the three OPP officers went back to their partners and all six fanned out in the parking lot.

By a few minutes before ten, everyone looked tense. Almost every head in the place was turned toward the highway, trying to spot the bus. The OPP officers all had their hands poised over their batons, but you could see from their faces that none of them actually wanted to have to use the batons against anyone, certainly not against any of the law-abiding citizens of East Hastings.

I looked out over the swelling crowd. Most people were milling around together, but there were a few people on the very fringes of the parking lot. Fence sitters, I decided — people who hadn't made up their minds one way or the other, or who were just here for the action that might erupt. Ross Jenkins was there, notebook in hand, as usual. He was probably here to cover Caleb's arrival for either the school newspaper or the local *Beacon*, where he had recently landed a part-time job. A few paces away from him stood a woman. She was old, quiet and still. I had no idea who she was.

Then, one by one, heads turned. Voices fell silent. OPP officers straightened up. I saw Levesque glance at Steve Denby. Then I turned my head and I saw it. The bus. Rolling right toward us.

CHAPTER THREE

Maybe the bus driver thought he was carrying anonymous royalty. Or maybe he knew that one of his passengers was notorious. Or maybe none of the above. But I bet he had never seen a crowd that big waiting for him at Benny's. Levesque waved down the driver before he made the turn into the lot. The bus door swung open and Levesque climbed inside. I saw him talking to the driver. Then the door closed again and the driver nosed the bus into the parking lot, at a snail's pace. People moved toward it, crowding around it before it had even stopped moving. From where I was standing, the driver looked tense.

When the bus finally came to a stop, Steve Denby and four of the OPP officers pushed their way to the front door and formed two lines, making a corridor between the door and the crowd. No one spoke a word as the bus door hissed open. A woman and a little girl stepped down onto the pavement and looked around. They seemed bewildered as they made their way down the double line of police officers. Then an old man climbed down and blinked at the crowd. He turned and held up his hand. An old woman — his wife, I guessed — emerged. She looked around nervously. They, too, walked between the two rows of police officers and cleared the edges of the crowd.

For another moment, nothing happened.

People glanced at one another, then strained forward, trying to see what was going on inside the bus. Finally someone stepped out. Levesque. The bus door closed behind him. A buzz went through the crowd. I didn't need Einstein's IQ to figure out what they were thinking: *Where's Caleb Darke?*

Levesque stood and scanned the crowd. He seemed to be looking for something. He stepped between two OPP officers and beckoned to someone. A man stepped forward. Daniel Tyson. Levesque talked to him. I was too far away to hear what he was saying. Daniel Tyson's head wagged back and forth. Whatever Levesque was saying, Mr. Tyson wasn't buying it.

Finally Levesque turned away from him. He said something to the OPP officer closest to him and then thumped on the bus door. He stood back as it swung open again. Levesque disappeared inside for a moment. Then he jumped back out, landing lightly, and moved ahead a step. Someone else came down from the bus. The crowd surged forward and the OPP officers had to strain to keep them back. People started yelling. I saw a woman in the crowd, Sarah Moran's mother. Her face was red, her mouth twisted, as she shouted at the tall, dark-haired man who had just stepped onto the pavement in Benny's parking lot.

Levesque's face was grim. He took the man — Caleb Darke — by the arm and led him through the crowd. Something flew through the air. Caleb ducked. So did Levesque. But it hit them anyway. Hit them and splattered. Eggs. Levesque brushed away the yolky mess. He never lost his grip on Caleb. The two columns of OPP officers stayed with them, forming a barrier against the crowd, until they reached Levesque's patrol car. He opened the back door and helped Caleb inside. Then he got inside too. The crowd swarmed around the car, pushing the OPP officers and Steve Denby aside.

"Geez," Eric said. "It's like they want to kill him or something."

I couldn't take my eyes off Levesque's patrol car. It was moving, but just barely. There were too many people pressed around it. The OPP officers were working at pulling them away, but gently. It looked to me like they were trying to avoid arresting anyone. Me, I would have been out there in full riot gear inviting anyone who got in my way to spend the night in jail.

Finally the car cleared the parking lot. The shouting stopped when it disappeared around the corner. I took another long, hard look at the mob. I wanted to know who was there. I wanted to recognize those people when I saw them again, and I wanted them to know that I recognized them.

Finally people dribbled away, the bus left, the OPP cars drove away and Steve Denby went back to the office.

When I turned to look at Eric, Kyle was already halfway across the parking lot and headed for the street. "Where's he going?" I said.

Eric looked at me as if my brains were leaking out of my head right before his eyes.

"He hasn't seen his brother for eight years, except for during prison visiting hours and a couple of quick trips to Toronto," he said. "Where do you think he's going?"

"Yeah? Well if he's so eager to see his brother, why wasn't he standing right up at the bus to greet him?" I said. "Why did he hang back way over here?"

Mr. Genius Jock didn't have an answer to that.

* * *

Eric left soon after. As I said goodbye to him, I spotted Ross standing near the main entrance to Benny's, staring out into space. I walked over to him, but had to say his name twice and then tap him on the shoulder to get his attention.

"You okay, Ross?" I said.

He shook his head as if he were trying to clear it. "I've seen a lot of things happen in this town," he said. "But I've never seen anything like that. My next-door neighbour was here. So was Mrs. Kinnear."

I had no idea who Mrs. Kinnear was.

"She was my kindergarten teacher," Ross said. "She must be at least sixty-five by now. She was here and she was *yelling* at Caleb Darke."

I sympathized with him. It had to be unnerving to see people you knew so well acting like members of a lynch mob. "People in crowds sometimes do things that they wouldn't do if they were alone," I said.

"I know," Ross said. The thought didn't seem to cheer him. "But Mrs. Kinnear used to read us *Winnie the Pooh*."

"The way people are carrying on, either Caleb Darke is Evil walking on two feet, or Terri Tyson is some kind of saint," I said.

"He was the kind of guy who always seemed to be in trouble," Ross said. "He was always getting into fights. I heard he beat up Terri's brother once."

"Caleb beat up Charles Tyson?"

Ross nodded. "Charles didn't want Caleb anywhere near his sister. You know how some people are about Native People. Charles especially."

Caleb's glossy black hair and Kyle's long black hair suddenly clicked into my brain. "Caleb and Kyle are Native?"

"Their mother was," Ross said. "Their father was white."

"Was?" I said. "You mean, they're both dead?"

Ross nodded again. "Kyle's father was killed in a hunting accident, just before Kyle was born. His mother died when he was three or four years old. He lives with his uncle, Thaddeus Darke." Ross said the name as if I should recognize it. I didn't.

"An old guy," he said. "Grey ponytail, leather hat. You can't help noticing him when he's in town."

"Drives a mostly rusted pickup?" I said.

Ross nodded.

Yeah, I'd seen him around. He looked like a refugee from the sixties, some old hippie who probably still grooved to Dylan and had fond memories of communes, crunchy granola and *Easy Rider*.

"That's Kyle's uncle, huh?" A guy like that made me look at Kyle in a whole new light. "What about Terri Tyson?"

"What about her?"

"Eric told me that she and Caleb had planned to get married."

"Eric," Ross said. "It figures."

"What's that supposed to mean?"

"Nothing."

Right. He sounded just like Phoebe. "Nothing" was bothering an awful lot of people all of a sudden. "What's up, Ross?" I asked.

He blew out a lungful of air that sounded more like an explosion than a sigh. "I remember what Terri was like before it happened," he said. "She baby-sat me sometimes. She was really pretty and a lot of fun. She'd show up with a bag full of crayons and colouring books and balloons. She knew a million and one knock-knock jokes. And she could draw anything. I still have a bunch of cartoons she did for me. She was head of her class in school, too. And editor of the school newspaper."

Ross was the current editor.

"She was interested in all kinds of things and good at everything. She got a full scholarship to university. Except that by the time she graduated high school, she didn't want to go. She took a job in town instead, working for Jimmy Johnston."

"And you think that was because of Caleb?"

"That's what everybody said. She was in love

with him." He shook his head. "A lot of people never figured out what she saw in him. He dropped out of high school. He did seasonal work with a logging company when he wasn't doing odd jobs. He did some work for Jimmy Johnston too. And he spent a lot of time out in the bush with his grandfather or his uncle. And with his record . . . "

I studied Ross and glanced at the notebook in his hand. "Which side are you on, Ross?"

"What do you mean?" Ross said, blinking.

One thing I've learned about Ross is that when you ask him a question that makes him feel uncomfortable, his eyelids go into overdrive. *Blinkety-blink–blink–blink* — like he's a signalling machine, except that he's really trying to avoid sending any messages. "It's a simple question," I said. "Do you think Caleb should stay or go?"

Blinkety–blink–blink–blink.

"You and Kyle are the same age," I said. I tried to picture Ross and Kyle as nine-year-olds. Ross came out pretty much the way he was now — scrawny, kind of nerdy, probably carrying a book and a notepad with him everywhere he went. I had a little more trouble envisioning Kyle as the silent, downward-looking guy he was today. I'm not sure why. "I bet you were in some of the same classes."

"If you grow up in this town, when you're in elementary school you're in the same class as everyone your age, at least once. Usually more often," he said. He sounded overly defensive. "So?"

"Just asking. It's no big deal."

He glowered at me, like he didn't trust me.

"Eric says that Caleb said he didn't do it," I said.

"There it is," Ross said, like he'd been expecting me to lob a mud ball at him, and I hadn't disappointed him.

"There what is?"

"I saw you with Eric. His uncle was Caleb's lawyer so, of course, he's convinced Caleb is innocent. And you're even worse. You think *everyone* in prison is innocent. First it was Jonah's dad . . . "

Jonah Shackleton's father. A whole other story.

"Not the best example," I said.

"Whatever," Ross said. "True or false: Eric's got you believing that Caleb was wrongfully convicted."

Usually I'm pretty calm, although there are some people who might dispute that. I'm calm right up to the point when someone says something that pokes me right where I don't want to be poked.

"First of all," I said, "nobody *gets* me believing anything — not Eric, not anybody. I'm perfectly capable of thinking for myself — "

"Whoa," Ross said, holding up his hands like he thought he was going to have to defend himself against a physical attack. "Struck a nerve, huh?"

"And second of all," I said, "you know as well as I do that sometimes the justice system doesn't work the way it should. I mean, you have to wonder — "

"No way, Chloe." He started to back away from me.

"No way what?"

"I'm not buying it."

"Not buying what?"

"Whatever you're selling."

"I'm not selling anything."

"Yeah. Sure. You were just *wondering*."

"Well, think about it, Ross. Caleb was convicted of aggravated assault and sentenced to eight years. He could have been out on parole a long time ago if he'd taken responsibility for what he did. But he refused. Instead, he stayed in prison until they had to let him go. If he really had done it, why wouldn't he just say, 'I'm sorry, I'm going to turn my life around,' and get himself out on parole? Why would he stay in prison a day longer than he had to?"

"Uh-huh," Ross said. "In other words, what you're saying is the fact that he was in prison proves that he's innocent."

I opened my mouth to say, *No, that's not what I'm saying at all.* Except that, in a way, it was. And how much sense did that make?

CHAPTER FOUR

Everyone knew Terri Tyson. Even if they didn't know her personally, they recognized her as the woman in the wheelchair who liked to spend a couple of afternoons a week at the daycare centre attached to the United Church. I often passed by there on my way home from school. If it was early enough and the weather was warm and the kids were outside playing, I'd see Terri watching, her wheelchair parked to one side of the playground. On warm spring days or crisp clear winter days, I'd see her in the big park adjacent to the arena. She'd be on the sidelines of a soccer game or a baseball game, or she'd be sitting with a blanket over her knees at the edge of the skating rink, watching boys play hockey or listening to the music blare as skaters swirled around and around.

I knew she was Charles's sister. I knew she had suffered some kind of brain injury. But I hadn't known the cause of that injury. I hadn't known that she was once engaged to Kyle Darke's brother. And I sure hadn't known that Caleb Darke had served time because of what had happened to her. I'd never even got close to her.

I parted company with Ross and walked back along Centre Street, trying to think how I was going to spend the rest of my Saturday. I could go to the library and study — exams were barely a month away. I could go home and work on the half-dozen projects I had due between now and the end of term. Or I could put all of that off until tomorrow and go downtown instead. I still sort of smiled when I thought of "downtown" and East Hastings in the same breath. The commercial centre of East Hastings consists of fewer than ten blocks of stores, businesses and restaurants. It takes twenty minutes, at a relaxed pace, to stroll from one end to the other. I opted for procrastination and began that stroll.

I slowed down in front of the first bank I passed, only because Eric had told me it was the one that Daniel Tyson managed. I tried to picture the red-faced man I'd seen yelling at Levesque in front of the police station and again in the parking lot at Benny's, sitting in a banker's office, doing whatever it is bank managers do. It was like trying to fit together pieces from two different jigsaw puzzles. Then, just as I was *thinking* of Daniel Tyson, I saw him. He was outside the Medical Building — a low-rise building that housed a couple of doctors' offices, a dentist's office, an optometrist and a physiotherapist, all situated over a ground-floor pharmacy. He pushed off from the car he'd been leaning against and propelled himself toward the building. The door swung open before he reached it and a wheelchair rolled out, guided by a middle-aged woman. In the wheelchair was a much younger woman. Her head lolled a little to one side and she slumped forward slightly. She would have been pretty if her face hadn't been so slack and if her posture had been better. It was Terri Tyson.

I hung back and tried not to look like I was staring, even though I was doing my best to get a good look at the woman who was at the centre of everything I had just seen. I wondered how aware she was of what was going on.

"So?" Mr. Tyson said.

The woman behind the wheelchair was Mrs. Tyson. Her face was pale. More than anything, she looked tired. But she smiled at Terri and said, "She did very well today. She even managed a few words."

A few words? Terri had been injured more than eight years ago. A few words didn't seem like much progress in all that time.

"Maybe this new therapy will work," Mrs. Tyson said. "Maybe she'll be able to communicate with us again."

"That would be so good," Daniel Tyson said. He reached down and patted Terri's hand.

What happened next made me jump. Terri yowled as if she had been scalded. She jerked back in her chair, her head flopping back. She was looking up at her father — or maybe she was just looking up, I don't know — and she yowled again.

Mrs. Tyson's face turned red. She glanced up and down the street and, sure enough, a few people were looking in her direction. Judging from the expressions on their faces, they were doing the same thing I was — wondering what was going on.

"You know she doesn't like to be touched," Mrs.

Tyson hissed at her husband.

Mr. Tyson had jumped back and was now as still as a block of wood. His hand — the one that had touched Terri — hung at his side. As he stared at his daughter, his eyes glistened. It didn't take much to imagine that if he were alone, he might have started to cry. No wonder he hated Caleb Darke. His beautiful daughter had lost everything, all because she had fallen in love.

Mrs. Tyson knelt down in front of Terri. "It's okay, honey," she said. "It's okay. We're going to go home right now, okay? Mama's going to take you home."

Terri stopped yowling, but she still fidgeted and seemed agitated. Mrs. Tyson pushed the wheelchair to the car standing at the curb. She opened the door and bent down to talk to Terri again before struggling to get her inside while Mr. Tyson stood to one side, watching. Only after Terri and her mother were safely stowed in the back seat did Mr. Tyson circle around to the driver's door and get in. As I watched them drive away, I wondered how I would feel if Terri was my mother or my sister. I wondered how I would feel if the person who'd done this to her was now free to walk the streets, while the person I loved was confined to a wheelchair. I wondered if maybe I would have reacted the same way Mr. Tyson had. But you can't know what you'll do in some situations until you're actually in them yourself.

* * *

I bought a new pair of jeans and two T-shirts on sale at one of the stores on Centre Street — and dreamed about all the boutiques and shops I used to be able to browse in, back home in Montreal. A year ago, I could have spent an entire day shopping. Now it was a miracle if I could make an East Hastings shopping trip last more than an hour. There were only so many stores. And the nearest mall was sixty kilometres away. Still, I had managed to exhaust my money before running out of things I wanted to buy. So I headed over to Canadian Tire to hit Mom up for an advance on my allowance.

She held up five fingers when she saw me come through the front door. I knew what that meant: she had her break in five minutes and I had to wait. I sighed and started to wander up and down the aisles. I know that, for a lot of people, a trip to Canadian Tire is a little piece of heaven — all that hardware, all those automotive accessories, all that sports equipment. I am not one of those people. But when you have time to kill, what are you going to do?

I began with housewares on the far right of the main door and worked my way through small appliances, lighting and storage solutions. When I turned the corner into the seasonal aisle — which at this time of year was stocked with Rollerblades, kneepads, footballs, baseballs, basketballs, skipping ropes, sidewalk chalk, everything for your outdoor amusement — I saw a small boy trying to climb up the shelving. If he had been a monkey, he might have succeeded. But he was just a small, uncoordinated boy, so I wasn't surprised when his foot slipped. The next thing I knew, he had lost his handhold, too. I started forward, even though I had no chance of reaching him before he hit the floor. It was just instinct.

Then a man appeared — he hadn't been there, and then there he was, so I guess his reflexes were better than mine. He scooped the little boy into his arms. The boy seemed startled to find himself looking into a weather-beaten face under a wide-brimmed leather hat. A grey ponytail hung down the man's back. Thaddeus Darke.

His pale blue eyes sparkled and the skin around them crinkled as he said something in a soft voice to the little boy. The boy nodded and Mr. Darke smiled. The little boy pointed up — way up — to a display of soccer balls on the second shelf from the top. He directed Mr. Darke to the exact ball he wanted. Mr. Darke brought it down and was handing it to the boy when another man charged down the aisle and snatched the boy. The man glowered at Mr. Darke. He didn't speak. He whisked the boy away. The boy shrieked for his ball. I heard him crying long after he had disappeared from sight.

Mr. Darke stood still for a moment. His eyes met mine. Then he turned, put the ball back onto the shelf and walked back up the aisle, away from me. I wondered what Eric would have thought if he had seen what I had just witnessed. I wondered how he'd feel about living in East Hastings now.

I wandered back to Mom's checkout counter.

There was someone else at the register with her. Mom had mentioned that she was training a new cashier. This must be her.

"Chloe, I'd like you to meet Audrey Martin. Audrey, this is my daughter Chloe."

Audrey Martin smiled. She had a prominent gap between her top two front teeth. It gave her a kind of goofy look.

I nodded.

"Your mother's showing me the ropes," Audrey said. "Thank goodness. I had no idea a person had to know so much about nuts and bolts and nails and screws and . . . " She shook her head.

"Give it a week and you'll be numbed by boredom like the rest of us," Mom said with a laugh. She dug her keys out of her pocket, unlocked a small cupboard under the counter and pulled out her purse. "Here," she said, handing me a couple of bills.

* * *

That night, just as we were about to have dessert — ice cream, with butter tarts that Phoebe had made — the phone rang.

"I'll get it," I said.

It was Steve Denby. I carried the phone to the dining-room door and waved it at Levesque. He got up from the table, took it from my hand and walked back into the kitchen, listening to whatever Steve was saying. When he hung up, he came back into the dining room.

"I'm sorry," he said to Mom, "but I have to go."

Mom looked worried. She always looked worried

when Levesque got called away, even though the worst thing that had ever happened to him was a nasty black eye from a drunk who'd taken a swing at him.

"Trouble?" she asked.

"A disturbance at the Tysons'," he said. He kissed her on the cheek.

Phoebe and I looked at each other. I knew we were thinking the same thing: *What kind of disturbance? And does it involve Caleb Darke?*

Phoebe was stacking dishes in the dishwasher, which meant that I was supposed to be scrubbing pots, pans and other non-dishwasher-able items in the sink. Instead, I was thumbing through the slim East Hastings telephone directory.

"Hey!" Phoebe said. She peered over my shoulder to see what I was up to.

Tyson, D. There it was. I memorized the address. It would take me fifteen minutes to get there if I speed-walked.

"I'll clean up for you tomorrow," I said to Phoebe. "Alone."

"If Dad sees you, he'll be angry," she said.

"Tomorrow night *and* the next night," I said. "I promise."

Phoebe jammed the last few plates into the dishwasher.

"Mom, I just remembered that I have to drop off my biology notes for Jenny," Phoebe said. "She missed class yesterday and she's going up to her grandmother's tomorrow. I'll finish cleaning up as soon as I get back, I promise."

"And I'm meeting Ross at the movies," I called to Mom. "I won't be late. I promise."

"Be careful," Mom said. She always said that: *Be careful.* Like danger was lurking behind every sleepy East Hastings corner in the form of a mugger or a drug dealer.

"We will," I said. Then I waited for the inevitable question.

"How are you getting home?"

Phoebe rolled her eyes. "Jenny lives five minutes away," she said. "And it's not even close to being dark."

"Ross will bring me home," I said. This would be news to Ross — assuming I even ran into him — but it satisfied Mom.

We ran, walked, ran, panted, walked and jogged our way down our street, across the field and the railroad tracks, across another field and into the town proper where the Tysons lived.

We were prepared to hang back in the shadows when we got there, so that Levesque wouldn't see us. It turned out that we needn't have worried. There must have been a couple of dozen people crowded out on the road and the sidewalk in front of the Tysons' house, all doing what Phoebe and I had come to do. All watching.

Two East Hastings patrol cars were pulled up in front of the house. I saw Steve Denby standing in the doorway of the Tyson house, blocking it. It was hard to tell whether he was keeping someone inside from leaving, or all the people outside from entering. When I peered around, looking for someone who could tell me what was going on, I recognized quite a few faces. None of them looked friendly. Then, at the darkest fringe of the lawn, I saw Kyle. Even when his brother was the main event, Kyle was a sideline kind of guy.

Steve Denby stepped aside to let someone pass. It was Caleb Darke. He was being escorted out of the house, in handcuffs, by Levesque. Someone in the crowd yelled, "Send him back to prison!" I turned, but couldn't tell who had shouted. People pushed forward, closing in on Levesque. Steve did his best to keep the crowd at bay, but there was only one of him. He looked tense. Levesque had a grip on Caleb with his left hand. His right hand hovered near his baton. He didn't look as tightly coiled as Steve, though. He peered at the faces in the crowd one by one, as if memorizing them. When his eyes met mine, my cheeks burned and I felt ashamed that I was there.

I turned to where Phoebe had been standing, but she wasn't there anymore. Little Miss Perfect — she had probably cut out before Levesque could spot her. Frankly, I was surprised she had decided to tag along in the first place.

Someone — Charles Tyson — raced out of the house and hurtled past Steve Denby. He ran directly at Caleb, one arm raised. Steve called out to Levesque, who whirled around and inserted himself between Caleb and the oncoming Charles.

"Step back, Charles," he said.

"Stay away from my sister!" Charles said, jabbing a finger at Caleb. "And you," he said to Levesque, "keep him away from here."

Levesque didn't move. Neither did Caleb.

"Go back into the house, Charles," Levesque said. He nodded at Steve, who came forward and touched Charles on the arm.

Charles stood his ground a moment, then turned and stormed back inside. I wondered what Mom would have thought if she'd seen the hatred in her boss's eyes.

"This town doesn't need people like you!" someone in the crowd yelled. A few others shouted their agreement. But although everyone kept close, no one actually tried to block Levesque. He marched Caleb down the driveway to one of the patrol cars, eased him into the back seat and shut the door. Steve slid in behind the wheel. They sat there, Steve in the front and Caleb in the back, while Levesque went back up to the house. He was inside for about five minutes, according to my watch. It seemed a lot longer, though. Finally he came out, walked to the second squad car and got inside. The two cars drove off, Steve's first, followed by Levesque's. The crowd milled around for a little longer, then gradually dispersed.

It was too early for me to go home — after all, I was supposed to be at the movies with Ross. So instead I walked downtown and went into Stella's Great Home Cooking for a coffee. There are two sections of seating in Stella's. At the front, there are tables near the window and a long counter with a dozen stools for people who are grabbing a quick coffee or who want to be part of the running gossip session that goes on all day. Retired people, people who aren't working and people on lunch breaks all make a point of passing through to catch up on local news. Along one side, and reaching into the back, are two long rows of booths. That's where you go if you want privacy.

I sat at the counter. A couple of old men anchored one end. On my other side were two younger guys and a young woman — the girlfriend of one of them, I think. All of the tables in the front window were occupied — two by groups of men, three by groups of women, and the other two, mixed. As far as I could tell, they all shared the same conversational agenda — Caleb Darke.

"He should have been charged with attempted murder."

"If the Crown attorney who decided on the charges actually lived in this town, if he knew Terri, maybe he'd have made a different decision."

"Why did he have to come back here? Doesn't he know he's not wanted?"

"Why was he even *allowed* to come back here? Don't the authorities care about Terri and how she feels?"

"The system is crazy. It's more concerned about the criminals than the victims."

"Why does Terri have to be in position where she

faces her attacker every day? Why isn't there some kind of law against that?"

If a stranger had stumbled into Stella's, he would have concluded that no one in town supported Caleb Darke's right to return home after paying his debt to society. But maybe all the people who weren't in Stella's had a different view of things. It was possible. Anything was possible.

I paid for my coffee and walked down to the East Hastings police station. Steve Denby was coming out as I was going in. He looked tired.

"Long day, huh?" I said.

He offered me a wan smile. "I can't remember the last time I was ready to go home and go to bed this early," he said. He glanced back over his shoulder and shook his head. "A friendly warning, Chloe. He's in a bad mood."

Levesque was sitting at his desk, staring at the screen of his computer. He glanced up when the door clicked shut behind me. He did not greet me with a smile, or say one word. Steve was right. *Somebody was grumpy.* But if I retreated without saying anything, I'd look like a coward. And I don't like to do that.

"Did you arrest Caleb?" I asked.

Levesque just kept looking at me. He had eyes that were deep brown in some lights, black in others. When he turned them on Mom, they were soft and sweet, like chocolate. When he was contemplating some case he was working on, they were dark, like a well or a pit. When he was angry, they were hard and black, like coal. Tonight they could have fuelled a furnace. So I was surprised when he answered, instead of giving me his cop evil eye.

"He's in back, thinking things over." There were a couple of cells in back.

"I was over at Stella's," I said cautiously. Just because he hadn't snapped at me yet didn't mean he wasn't going to. "People don't seem happy that he's back in town."

Levesque leaned back in his chair. "He served his time. He's not even on parole. The man's entitled to live where he wants."

That was the part I didn't get. "But why would he want to live here when it's so obvious he's not welcome?"

Levesque glanced at his computer screen for a moment. Then he looked at me. "Do me a favour? Tell your mother I'm going to be home late."

It was clear I wasn't going to get any information out of him. I was about to leave when the door opened behind me. Levesque straightened up in his chair. I turned to see a man in a wide-brimmed leather hat, with hair pulled back in a silver ponytail. He wasn't anywhere near as big as Levesque, but his shoulders were broad and he strode across the room with the energy of a man a fraction of his age. He came to a stop when he reached Levesque's desk. He laid his large hands on the edge of the desk and leaned forward to squint at Levesque.

"I came for my nephew," he said.

"You must be Thaddeus Darke," Levesque said.

Mr. Darke didn't answer. Levesque stood up slowly, unfolding himself from his chair bit by bit until he towered over the smaller man. "I'm Louis Levesque," he said, extending a hand.

Mr. Darke looked at Levesque's outstretched hand, but didn't reach for it.

Levesque glanced at me. "Run along, Chloe," he said.

"No need for that," Mr. Darke said. "I'm not staying."

Levesque glanced at me again. I backed up a few steps as if I were intending to leave — which I wasn't.

"I came for my nephew," Mr. Darke said again, louder this time, his voice edged with anger. "He's done nothing wrong."

"He forced his way into the Tyson place," Levesque said, the calm in his voice a vivid contrast to the bitterness in Mr. Darke's. "He gave me no choice but to charge him."

"It's them you should be charging, not Caleb," Mr. Darke said. "All he wanted was to see his Terri. That's all."

His Terri?

"As I understand it, Caleb and Terri are no longer engaged," Levesque said.

"That was *their* doing," Mr. Darke said. He must have meant the Tysons. "Caleb would marry that girl in a minute."

I saw a hint of surprise in Levesque's eyes.

"The fact remains that Caleb forced his way into

the Tyson home. That's an offence, Mr. Darke. I'm going to release him, but he'll have to sign a promise to appear and an undertaking to stay away from the Tyson house — and from the Tysons, including Terri. If he doesn't abide by the conditions of that undertaking, he's going to find himself in serious trouble. Do you understand?"

Mr. Darke glowered up at Levesque.

"Mr. Darke, do you understand?"

"I understand," Mr. Darke said, all but spitting the words at Levesque.

"Fine," Levesque said. "I'm going to get Caleb. I want you and him both to read the undertaking. Once he signs it and the promise to appear, you can take him home." Levesque came out from behind his desk. That's when he noticed that I was still skulking around the door.

"Chloe," he said, "go home."

Chapter Five

Monday is not my favourite day, and morning is not my favourite time of day. So I never get out of bed with great expectations on a Monday, especially not during the school year; especially not with final exams creeping closer and closer. I pretty much expect Monday mornings to be painful. This particular Monday morning did not fail to live down to my abysmal expectations.

I should have foreseen it. After all, I'd had an omen, namely that as East Hastings Regional High loomed into view, the first thing — think *insect* — that I saw was Rick Antonio. Yuck. Then I widened my focus. Rick, Brad Hudson and some of the other jocks had formed a rough circle on the playing field. A bunch of other kids clustered around them. I'd been in high school long enough to know what that meant.

My first instinct was to stay away. Circles like that are like people slowing down on the highway to gawk at an accident scene. I didn't want to be one of those losers. But where there's an accident, there's usually a victim. And where there's Rick Antonio, there's definitely a bully. A minute later I was muscling my way through a line of my fellow students.

Kyle Darke was standing in the middle of the circle, a brownish beanpole with a scraggle of long black hair that hung over his face as he stared

44

down at the ground. Opposite him — no surprise — was Rick Antonio. Between them — *big* surprise — was my kid sister.

"Just try it," Phoebe said, her eyes fixed fiercely on Rick. "Get lost. Before I decide to report you."

My little sister was threatening a guy who was taller and heavier and stronger than her, and who was one hundred percent jock. Kyle stood where he was, looking at the ground. Maybe he was paralysed with fear. Maybe he didn't care. Maybe he was high on something. I don't know. But he wasn't moving, and he didn't seem to be paying any attention to what was going on around him.

Rick nudged Brad and they both laughed. Some kids around them laughed too. Some didn't. Others just watched.

Then Rick made a big mistake. He grabbed Phoebe by the arm. "Get out of the way," he said, yanking at her.

Phoebe tried to hold her ground, but Rick had the advantage. I could see that she was trying hard to be strong, but she'd been dislodged from her position. Then Brad grabbed her too and pulled her even further away. Kyle wasn't doing anything, so I strode into the middle of the circle.

"You got a problem, Rick?" I said. Like I even needed to ask.

Rick smiled when he looked at me, but there was nothing friendly in the expression. He didn't like me. He never had and probably never would. I didn't care.

"Your sister doesn't know how to mind her own business," he said, giving me a once-over. "Looks like you don't either. Kyle and I were just having a private conversation."

I glanced at Kyle, who was doing a good imitation of the Washington Monument — tall and silent and made of stone. Maybe he didn't care, but he wasn't doing himself any favours. People already thought he was weird. Now they were going to think he was gutless, too. And what was I supposed to do? What could anybody do for a guy who wouldn't stand up for himself?

"I was asking Kyle here how come he and his wannabe-killer big brother don't make things easier on everyone and just go back to the reserve," Rick said.

Kyle's head bobbed up at the mention of his brother. At first I thought he was looking at Rick, but then I tracked what his eyes were focused on. It wasn't Rick at all, but something — some*one* — beyond Rick. I looked, too — at Brad and the rest of the jocks, at kids who sat in some of my classes, at Dean Abbott and Sarah Moran and Vanessa Sutherland. To their credit, each one of them lowered their eyes to the ground. Then I saw Ross. At first he was looking right back at Kyle, and his mouth hung open for a moment, as if he were going to say something. Then it closed and, like everyone else, Ross shifted his eyes down to the ground. When he did, I felt disappointed.

"Come on, Kyle," I said. I caught one of his hands

in mine. It was cool and dry. He didn't resist.

Phoebe wrestled herself free from a couple of Rick's jock friends, and grabbed Kyle's other hand.

"What a loser," Rick said loudly. "Got a couple of *girls* fighting his fights for him."

Naturally, the jocks thought this was highly amusing. Just as naturally, I didn't. First of all, I didn't care for the twist he gave to the word *girls*, as if we were a couple of kittens going up against a big he-grizzly bear. Second, technically this wasn't even a fight. At least it wasn't until Rick started forward, secure in the knowledge that mere *girls* weren't going to offer Kyle much protection.

I think that's why I did it — because he seemed so sure. Just as he was about to jump Kyle, I balled my right hand into a fist and I plowed it right into Rick's unsuspecting belly.

I knew it was wrong even before I made contact. The feeling that I was doing something terrible disappeared momentarily when I was treated to a look of pure astonishment on Rick's face. It returned when I saw him double over, which, I guess, proves that I have what Mom calls a moral compass, that handy little item that lets you distinguish between right and wrong. That compass got a little confused when at least half the crowd let out a yell of approval, but righted itself with the help of Mr. Moore — no relation to Eric Moore, as Eric is always pointing out. Mr. Moore is one of East Hastings Regional's two vice-principals. He waded into the crowd with Mr. Mowat, who was also Rick's football coach, which meant this could go either way.

First Mr. Moore dispersed the crowd. Then he told Phoebe, Kyle and me to stay put. He turned his attention to Rick, who promptly deposited his breakfast on Mr. Moore's right shoe. Looked like scrambled eggs to me. Maybe bacon, too. I saw little brown bits. Mr. Moore turned and gave me a look that screamed, *Detention for life!*

The bell rang before everything was sorted out. Mr. Moore talked briefly to Rick's friends and then sent them into school. He took Kyle aside and talked to him, then to Phoebe, who talked back energetically. Then they too were dismissed. This left Rick, Mr. Moore, Mr. Mowat and me out on the field. Mr. Moore nodded at Mr. Mowat, who led Rick toward the school. Rick's face was a lovely cream colour. He walked slightly hunched over. Mr. Moore watched them go before turning to me.

"You are familiar with the zero-tolerance policy, aren't you?" he said.

Yeah, I was familiar with it. I nodded.

"So you know what this means?" he said.

Yup. It meant that I should have let Rick take the first swing. Then he would have been the one looking at an automatic suspension.

"Even if I decide to be nice and call what you just did *fighting*, that's a one-day minimum suspension," he said. "If I call it what it really was, physical assault, that's three days. *Minimum.*"

"Rick was giving Kyle a hard time," I said in my

defence. "My sister was sticking up for Kyle when I got here, and Rick was giving *her* a hard time, too. What was I supposed to do?"

Mr. Moore crossed his arms over his chest and shook his head as he looked at me.

"Okay," I said. "Okay, so I should have gone to the office and reported what was going on. I shouldn't have taken matters into my own hands." Geez, did every guy in a position of authority have to act like a guy in a position of authority? (Which usually meant acting like a wise adult who was trying, almost always in vain, to teach a lesson to a kid — usually the hard way.) "But you should have a zero-tolerance policy on 'just standing around watching some guy being persecuted because of something his brother did and has already paid for,'" I said.

Mr. Moore let out such a long, loud sigh that if he'd had any hair near the front of his head, it would have blown straight up in the air. "Someone as sensible as you should learn to keep a tight grip on her temper," he said at last.

I was tempted to glance around to see if someone — someone *sensible* — had crept up behind me and *that's* who he was talking to. But I didn't and it wasn't. He was talking to me.

"Go to class now," he said, "before I change my mind."

"Yes, sir."

"And, Chloe? This is a once-in-a-lifetime pass. You got that?"

"Yes, sir."

* * *

At lunchtime, I headed for the school newspaper office, where I'm on staff as a reporter. The job wasn't entirely my choice, but I didn't entirely hate it, either.

Phoebe cornered me just as I reached the stairs to the basement, where the newspaper office is located. "Thanks," she said. Her expression seemed to be one of admiration, but because she was my sister, I knew I had to be misreading it. Probably she had a fever. Maybe she was delusional. "You wouldn't believe the things Rick was saying before you got there," she said. Her eyes glistened with pent-up tears.

"Yeah, I would," I said. "I know Rick." I had been stupid enough to go out with him. In my defence, I'd been smart enough to be that stupid only once. "Forget about him, Pheebs. He's an idiot."

"People just let him say it," Phoebe said, getting to the thing that was really bothering her. "No one stuck up for Kyle."

"Yeah, well, people are stupid sometimes. Or they're cowards. Or they think it's fine so long as *they're* not the ones being picked on by guys like Rick. Whatever. You can't do anything about *people*, Phoebe. The only person you can do anything about is you."

She stared at me as if I'd suddenly grown a second head.

"What?" I said.

"Nothing."

"*What?*"

"I just wanted to thank you, that's all," she said. "Kyle's not weird. He's just shy. And sad." She said this as if it were an indisputable fact, not the idle speculation of a disinterested bystander. I wondered how she knew so much about Kyle Darke.

"I guess everyone can use a friend, right?" I said.

She nodded and offered me a wan little smile.

* * *

Ross saw me enter the worldwide headquarters of the *East Hastings Herald*. I know he did. As editor, he had his own cubbyhole of an office in one corner of the large room that served as the newspaper's nerve centre. He glanced up from his computer screen when he heard the door open. But he quickly looked down again, hunching forward in his chair, as if he were completely engrossed in whatever he was writing. Yeah, well, you can fool some of the people some of the time . . .

"Hey, Ross," I said from the door to the cramped editor's office.

"I'm kind of busy, Chloe," he said, staring as steadfastly at his computer screen as he had stared at the ground out on the playing field. "Deadlines, you know."

"I never acted too busy to speak to you or help you out when you were in trouble," I said.

Ross is a stand-up kind of guy, firmly entrenched on the honour roll, engaged in all the right extracurriculars for someone whose ambition is law school. Or maybe journalism school — it depends what day of the week it is and what he's been thinking about when you ask him. But, upstanding or not, he'd still managed to land himself in some real mud pits in the year that I'd known him.

He clicked on *Save* before swivelling his chair around to face me. "Okay," he said, "what can I do for you?"

"Not for me. For Kyle."

Ross blinked at me. I think the look he was going for was a question mark, a great big *huh?* of innocent befuddlement. He didn't quite pull it off, though.

"Come on, Ross," I said. "When Rick was giving Kyle a hard time, Kyle was looking at you like he was disappointed to see you standing there. You two used to be friends, didn't you?"

Ross is the kind of guy who should never play poker or, if he does, should never try to bluff. He was shaking his head in denial, but every other part of his body was screaming yes, yes, yes! His cheeks turned a slow crimson. His eyes looked everywhere but at me. He crossed his arms over his chest, a classic defensive pose.

"Phoebe hardly knows him," I said. "He's in one of her classes. But she stuck up for him. How come you didn't?"

When he saw I wasn't buying denial, he decided to try selling me a little indignation.

"Where do you get off, coming in here and accusing me of . . . of . . . "

"Cowardice?" I said helpfully. "Turning your back on a friend in need?"

"Kyle Darke is *not* my friend."

"He was, though," I said, every bit as sure as Phoebe had been when she declared that Kyle wasn't weird. "What happened? Did you dump him when his brother got sent to prison?"

Ross sprang to his feet. "You always think you know everything," he said. "Right from the start, you've always had the attitude that *you're* so smart and *we're* a bunch of backward, prejudiced hicks who haven't got a clue what's going on in the world."

Whoa! Talk about hitting a nerve. "Fine," I said. "Prove me wrong. Tell me what happened between you and Kyle."

"Nothing happened."

"One day he was your friend, the next day he was off the list? Just like that?"

Ross glanced past me into the outer office. Half a dozen *Herald* staffers were out there — some talking, some banging away at computer keyboards, all of them pretending to have no interest in what Ross and I were talking about. Well, almost all of them. Eric was standing in the middle of the room, looking at Ross. Looking at him with an expression of pure disdain. Ross reached past me and shut the door to his office.

"We were in school together," he said.

"From what I've heard, everybody up here was in school with everybody else," I said. Ross himself had told me that. "But that doesn't make everyone friends."

Ross slumped into his swivel chair. "So we hung out together sometimes when we were kids. So what?"

"You tell me."

Ross looked down at the grey tile floor for a moment. "You know how it is," he said. "People start talking, especially in a place like this where everybody knows somebody who knows somebody else. You've heard of 'six degrees of separation'? Up here, it's two, maybe three, maximum. And when the charges against Caleb turned out to be aggravated assault, the whole town went nuts. Everyone — and I mean everyone, Chloe — thought he should have been charged with attempted murder. You think what happened at the bus stop on Saturday was bad? You should have seen the crowd that turned out at the police station when it got out, what Caleb had been charged with. And Caleb wasn't even being held here, he was being held in Sudbury. I heard the Darkes' place was trashed, too."

A week or so ago, I would have found it hard to imagine an angry mob in East Hastings. Now it didn't seem so far-fetched.

"Kids aren't immune to stuff like that," Ross said. "They hear their parents talk and they take that to school with them." He shrugged. "I don't know, I just sort of stopped hanging out with him. Geez, Chloe, I was eight years old when Caleb was sent away. And Terri was at my house the night before it happened." His voice got quieter. "She was different that night. Even I could see that something was bothering her."

"I heard Caleb supposedly attacked her because she was going to break up with him. Do you think that's what was on her mind, the fact that she was going to dump him?"

Ross shook his head. "I don't know. She didn't discuss her love life with me. But, yeah, I guess that was it. Everyone said they were a real-life Romeo and Juliet. The Tysons hated Caleb. They wanted Terri to go away to university. They wanted better for her than Caleb."

I flinched when I heard the word *better*. Ross must have caught it, too, because his cheeks and ears turned pink again.

"You know what I mean," he said.

I did, and I didn't approve, but I bit my tongue.

"What I remember most," he said, "was that she was sitting on the couch while I watched TV. She never used to do that. She never used to let me watch TV. We always did stuff together. But that night she just sat there on the couch. She had her backpack with her and she kept looking into it. She was acting like she had something really important in there, but she didn't."

Oh? "Did she tell you that?"

Ross's cheeks and ears turned pinker. "No," he said.

I can always tell when Ross is holding back. A five-year-old could figure it out. His eyes darted around the tiny office, looking at everything except me.

"You snooped, didn't you?" I said.

He couldn't have squirmed more if he'd been a worm on the end of a fishhook. I almost laughed out loud. Good old Ross. More than eight years after secretly rummaging through his baby-sitter's backpack, he still felt guilty.

"You did, didn't you, Ross?" I said, grinning.

"She usually paid a lot of attention to me when she was baby-sitting. That night she just kept fiddling with her backpack When she went to answer the phone, I peeked inside."

"And?"

"And nothing. Some books. A package wrapped in brown paper."

"Uh-huh?" I waited. "Come on," I said. "You opened it, didn't you?" I admit it, I was enjoying the agonized look of guilt on his face.

"It wasn't sealed or anything," he said. "And it wasn't anything special, either. Just an old jacket of some kind. It sure didn't explain why she was acting so . . . serious. And then the next night . . . " His voice trailed off. "When I see her now, sometimes I think about what she might be doing if things had been different."

We were silent for a moment, both thinking the same thing: *If only* . . .

Finally, Ross sighed. "So," he said, "how's your article going?"

I groaned. "How come I get all the loser stories?"

I had been assigned to write about the "friendly" rivalry between East Hastings Regional High and Morrisville and District Regional. I mean, who even cared? "I hate rah-rah school stories," I said.

I got no sympathy from Ross. But then, I hadn't expected any.

CHAPTER SIX

Mr. Mowat flagged me down on my way to my locker after school.

"Chloe, I've got a job for you," he said. Not, *Chloe, can you do me a favour?* Not even, *Please, Chloe.* Just, *Chloe, I've got a job for you.*

I waited.

"Drop by Canadian Tire," he said. "Charles Tyson is donating some first-aid guides to us and I want to hand them out in tomorrow's class. The team has a game up in Morrisville, so I can't pick them up myself."

"But — "

"Just ask for Charles. I told him I'd send someone by."

"Yeah, but — "

"I know, I know. Anyone else would have delivered them to the school. But Charles? Well, he's donating them. For that, we should be grateful. Be a sport," he said. "Pick them up and bring them to first period tomorrow." Without waiting for an answer, he shouldered his gym bag and headed down the hall.

I had a choice, of course. I could show up at school the next morning with first-aid guides, or I could show up without them.

I headed for Canadian Tire. When I got there, I walked the length of the store, peering up the aisles. Charles Tyson was the kind of store manager who liked to know what was going on in his little hardware kingdom. More often than not he was prowling the floor. Sure enough, I spotted him in the housewares aisle — *Irons and Toaster Ovens 30% Off!* A dozen or so other people, staff and shoppers, were clustered around him, listening to him argue with someone. Geez, I thought. It's like high school all over again. Then, as I got closer, I saw who he was arguing with. My mother.

"I'm not *demanding* anything," Mom was saying. Her face was flushed, a sure sign that she was excited or upset about something. "I'm just saying that I don't think that kind of remark is appropriate, under the circumstances."

"Is that right?" Charles said. He looked a little red in the face himself, and his voice sounded higher than usual. "Well, I don't think it's *appropriate* that our chief of police puts more effort into protecting criminals like Caleb Darke than innocent citizens like my sister. He's acting like Caleb is the victim here. Doesn't anyone care about Terri? Doesn't anyone care what happened to her? Nine years later, her life is still a mess and he gets to walk around here free as a bird, like nothing ever happened." He glanced at the people who were clustered around. Several of them nodded.

"*I* am not the chief of police," my mother said. She seemed to be forcing out her words through clenched teeth. "If you have something to say to him, by all means, say it. But you have no right to harass me all day for something that has nothing to do with me."

Charles Tyson had been harassing my mother?

"Oh, so now expressing an opinion is harassment?" Charles said, hands on hips, looking pretty cocky. But then, he had nothing to lose. He was the manager. He had hired and could fire everyone who worked in the store.

"Haranguing a person and blaming them for something that someone else did is harassment," someone said. I glanced around and saw Audrey Martin pushing through the little knot of shoppers. She came to a stop at my mother's side. "Sheila is right. If you have a problem with the chief of police, talk to the chief of police, don't ride his wife all day."

Charles zeroed in on her. "Do I need to remind you that you're still on probation?" he said.

Audrey stiffened. "You're threatening me?" she said. "In front of all these people?"

I don't know what *all these people* thought about what was going on, but a few of them shuffled uncomfortably. Maybe they agreed with Charles, and maybe they didn't. But it seemed to me that they didn't think my mother was to blame for anything.

Charles glared first at Audrey, then at my mother. Then he said, "Get back to work, the two of you."

My mother glared right back at Charles, holding him with her eyes for five, maybe ten seconds, before wheeling around and heading back to her checkout counter. She must have been blazingly angry, because she didn't even notice me standing there.

One elderly man patted Charles lightly on the back. A middle-aged woman squeezed his hand in what looked to me like sympathy. Then the crowd drifted away and Charles turned toward the door to his office. Great. Now what was I supposed to do? Follow him and ask for the first-aid guides Mr. Mowat had sent me for? Or forget the whole thing and spend the rest of the day trying to come up with some excuse to offer tomorrow?

I turned to look back at my mother and found that Audrey Martin had stood her ground and was glowering at Charles's back.

"What happened?" I asked her.

She clucked in disgust. "He's been going on all day about how *some people's husbands* show more concern for criminals than for their victims. It was pretty heavy-handed. Your mom didn't appreciate it."

Out of the corner of my eye I saw Charles disappear into his office and close the door.

"I have to go, Audrey," I said. I didn't really want to talk to Charles, not after he had been giving Mom a hard time. But it would be more trouble than I needed to show up at school tomorrow without the guides. I hurried down the far aisle of the store and knocked on the office door. From inside I heard a muffled "Come in." I pushed open the door just as Charles hung up the phone.

"Excuse me, Mr. Tyson," I said. I wanted to continue with something along the lines of, *If you ever talk to my mother like that again* . . . Instead, I choked back my anger and said, "Mr. Mowat sent me over to pick up some first-aid guides for school."

He looked blankly at me for a moment, as if he had no idea what I was talking about. Then he nodded, said, "Oh, yes," and picked up the phone again. "Ned," he said, "where are those first-aid guides?" He listened to whatever Ned was saying, then directed me to a storeroom at the back of the store. I thanked him and was happy to be on my way.

I collected the box of guides, which mercifully was much lighter than I had expected. As I was leaving the store, I stopped by Mom's checkout counter to see if she was okay.

"I'm fine," she said through tight lips. Fine, but angry, was my guess. "Do me a favour?" she said. "Don't mention this to Louis. He's already under enough pressure."

I promised I wouldn't.

* * *

I headed home with the box of first-aid guides. There were a couple of routes I could have taken. The one I chose took me past the United Church. Across the road from the church was a small cemetery. I saw someone inside it, kneeling in front of a headstone, but I didn't give it a second thought. I was more interested in what was happening in the playground. A horde of small children swarmed over the play equipment, closely supervised by two daycare workers. Sitting alone near the fence in her wheelchair, watching the little kids stream through the yard, was Terri Tyson.

I started to cross the road. As I did, I saw the man in the cemetery get to his feet and turn around. It was Caleb. He loped across the road, heading for the fence around the playground. My heart almost stopped in my chest. I glanced at the daycare workers, but they were too preoccupied with their charges to notice. Caleb looked at them, too, as if gauging how much danger they presented. Part of me wanted to shout a warning to the daycare workers. After all, Caleb had allegedly assaulted Terri before. He had forced his way into her house once already. He was headed toward her now.

But another part of me thought about what Eric had said — that Caleb was innocent. I kept walking, getting closer and closer, but he was nearer to Terri than I was. Then Terri turned her head and spotted him.

I don't know what I expected her to do, but I know what I *didn't* expect, and that was what she actually did. She smiled at Caleb. And Caleb smiled back. A soft, warm, tender smile. I glanced at the daycare workers, who were busy trying to sort out an argument among a group of five toddlers who all wanted a turn on the daycare's three tricycles.

Caleb walked up to the fence, right next to where Terri's chair was parked. He reached over it and laid one of his large, dark hands on one of her small, white ones. I remembered the last time I had seen someone touch her. Her father had put a hand on her arm and she had let out a yowl that had terrified me and alarmed both her mother and her father. *She doesn't like to be touched,* Mrs. Tyson had said.

But Terri wasn't yowling now. She was quiet and she continued to smile up at Caleb. I saw her mouth move. She was saying something to him. Or, at least, she was trying to. He leaned toward her, his eyes tight with concentration, as if he were trying to decipher her sounds. I remembered what Mrs. Tyson had said. Terri was learning to speak again. She had managed only a few words, her mother had said, but they represented progress. I wondered what those few words were and if she had just spoken them to Caleb.

When I turned again to check what the daycare workers were doing, I saw someone come around the side of the church. Mrs. Tyson. If she saw Caleb with Terri, she'd call Levesque. Caleb would be arrested again, and this time he'd be in big trouble. He had signed an undertaking. He had promised not to go anywhere near Terri. He had broken that promise.

Part of me thought that I should let him get caught. I should let him pay the price. But the unexpected joy on Terri's face made me act just like Caleb — it made me do the opposite of what I should have done. Instead of standing aside and letting him suffer the consequences of his actions, I ran to where he was standing, touched his arm and nodded toward the side of the church. He glanced at Mrs. Tyson. He squeezed Terri's arm and murmured something I didn't catch. Then he hurried away.

I took off too, to the cemetery side of the road where I could watch without seeming to watch. Mrs. Tyson went over to Terri and spoke to her. Terri didn't look at her mother. She was staring in the direction where Caleb had disappeared. It was only after it became obvious that Mrs. Tyson hadn't seen Caleb, hadn't even noticed him, that I realized I had been holding my breath. I had been rooting for him. I had been one hundred percent on Caleb Darke's side, and I wasn't entirely sure why.

I glanced around before leaving the cemetery. Caleb had been kneeling close to where I now stood. I wondered why. Had he been waiting there until he felt it was safe to make contact with Terri? Or had something else brought him here? Then I spotted the two headstones, side by side. One bore the name of Zachariah Darke. The other, Maria Sunday Darke. Kyle and Caleb's parents, judging from the dates and what Ross had told me.

Off to one side of Maria Darke's headstone was a third marker. The name on it was Matthew Sunday, "beloved father of Maria." According to the date on that stone, Matthew Sunday had died a few months before Terri was attacked and less than a year before Caleb was sentenced and sent to prison. Whether he deserved it or not, it seemed to me that Caleb had lost a lot in his life.

* * *

It ate at me all the way home. It ate at me during supper. It ate at me when I was supposed to be doing my homework. It ate at me so much that I thought fleetingly about talking to Levesque. But if I did that — if I even mentioned what was on my mind — he would probably have to do something about it, and I didn't want to get Caleb into trouble, especially after what I had seen. But still it ate at me until I thought it would devour me. That's when I found myself rapping on the door to Phoebe's room.

"Come in," she called cheerily. Good old Pheebs, always an optimist, always thinking there was a better-than-even chance that any knock at her door was an opportunity, some lucky once-in-a-lifetime offer.

But when I opened the door and she saw me standing there, her perky smile slipped and her eyes became guarded. "What?" she said. "I haven't been anywhere near your room, I swear."

"Can I talk to you for a minute?"

She eyed me the way a bear might eye a deer tied to a stake in the forest — looking for the pit, the foothold trap, the peril. Her nod was barely perceptible. I crossed the threshold and closed the door behind me.

"If I tell you something, you have to promise you won't tell anyone," I said. "And I mean anyone, Phoebe."

The apprehension vanished from her eyes, replaced with curiosity. I could almost see the wheels turning in her brain. *Anyone* meant Levesque. If I was hiding something from Levesque, then I must have done something wrong. If I told her what it was, she would have something to hold over my head. If she had something to use against me, she could also use that something to bargain with me.

I sat down on the edge of her bed and told her what I had seen in front of the medical building on Saturday, and then what I had seen at the church today.

"The thing is," I said — and this is what had been eating at me all evening — "if Terri really doesn't like to be touched, why did she react so calmly when Caleb touched her? And if he was the one who put her in that wheelchair, why did she smile at him the way she did?"

Phoebe thought about this for a few moments. "Maybe she didn't recognize him," she said slowly. "I mean, from what I heard, she suffered a lot of brain damage. Maybe she didn't realize it was him. Or maybe she doesn't remember what he did."

I suppose she could have been right. People lose all kinds of memories for all kinds of reasons. I suppose it's possible that a person could look with the purest love at someone who had hurt her so badly that her life was a shambles. Anything's possible. But I didn't believe it — not in this case. "Phoebe, you should have seen her. She smiled at him the way Mom smiles at Levesque."

"Louis," Phoebe said, sounding annoyed now. "If you don't want to call him Dad, you could at least call him by his first name."

"And Caleb acted the same way," I said. "If you'd

been there, you'd be thinking the same thing I am. Those two are in love with each other."

Phoebe didn't say anything. What could she say? She hadn't been there.

"You can't tell Levesque what I just told you," I said. "Caleb isn't supposed to go near Terri."

"I know," Phoebe said. She stared down at her desk for a moment. Her voice was small when she said, "Kyle says his uncle warned Caleb to stay away."

Kyle says? "Do you mean, you heard that's what Kyle says? Or do you mean, Kyle told *you* that?"

Phoebe raised her eyes slowly. What was that look on my little sister's face?

"Since when does Kyle Darke tell you things?" I said. What I was thinking was, *Since when does Kyle Darke even speak?*

"He's in my French class," was all she said.

"What else does he say?"

"That Caleb isn't listening to their uncle. That he says he's free now and he can do whatever he wants. And, Chloe?" Her voice trembled a little. "He said that what Caleb wants is to be with Terri. Kyle seems awfully worried about that. He thinks it's going to mean trouble."

What I was thinking, but what I didn't say, was, *Kyle is probably right.*

CHAPTER SEVEN

Mom was out at her book club when the doorbell rang. Phoebe was up in her room doing homework. Levesque was in the kitchen, taking leftovers out of the fridge. The man lived on leftovers. One of the perils of police work.

I was on the couch in the living room reading the assigned chapter in my history textbook, which made me closest to the front door, and which more or less obliged me to answer it. Well, me and Shendor, and she wasn't exactly helpful. I had to hold her collar to keep her from jumping on the angry-looking Daniel Tyson who was standing on our porch. He *demanded* to see the chief of police. I *told* him to wait outside — two could dance the let's-be-rude tango — and went to fetch Levesque.

He had just started to eat the fried chicken and potato salad that Mom had left for him. He looked longingly at the food on his plate, then plucked the napkin from his lap, dropped it onto the table and strode into the front hall. He closed both the inner and outer doors behind him. Nice try. It was a warm night and the windows were open, so all I had to do was hunker down on the couch where no one could see me.

The first voice I heard was Mr. Tyson's. "I demand that you do something," he was saying. My observation: *bank managers are very big on making demands.*

"He's signed an undertaking to stay away from Terri," Levesque said. He sounded tired. "He knows he'll be in trouble if he breaches that undertaking. I don't think he wants to make matters worse for himself."

"But that's just the point," Mr. Tyson said. "As I understand it, he talked to her today."

How did he know that? Had I been mistaken about Mrs. Tyson? Had she seen Caleb before he ran away? Had one of the daycare workers spotted him?

"As you understand it?" Levesque said. "So you didn't witness this yourself?"

"Well, no." Mr. Tyson spoke the two words with huge regret. "But my wife says that she has the impression, based on Terri's reaction when Darke showed up at the house the other night, that Terri had contact with him again."

"*Has the impression*? Can you be more specific, Mr. Tyson? Did Terri tell your wife she had spoken to Caleb?"

"My daughter doesn't speak many words as such," Mr. Tyson said.

"But she communicated this to your wife?"

"She was extremely agitated. In the course of trying to find out why, my wife mentioned Darke's name. Terri became even more agitated."

"I see."

I could imagine Levesque standing on the porch, digesting this information, running it through his legal filter.

"Did Terri actually say that Caleb made contact with her?"

I heard a little cluck of exasperation. "I've already told you. Communicating with Terri is, well, it's more or less one-sided. But my wife is very good at reading Terri and if she says Darke made contact with my daughter, then that's what happened. If he signed an undertaking to stay away from her, then you have grounds to arrest him. I know enough about police work to know that."

Another pause. Then, "Someone would have to make a complaint," Levesque said.

Another cluck. "I was under the impression I was doing just that."

"Someone who actually witnessed the incident would have to make the complaint," Levesque clarified.

"This is preposterous! This man beat my daughter almost to death. He destroyed her life and any chance she had for happiness. Now he's back threatening her again and you tell me you're not going to do anything about it?"

"I can't arrest someone without some kind of evidence that he's committed a crime," Levesque said evenly. "I'll go and talk to Caleb."

I heard a snort. "And I'm sure he'll tell you the truth and happily surrender himself to you!"

"At this point, all I can do — "

"You listen to me," Mr. Tyson said. "Next week I'm supposed to go down to Toronto for a meeting at bank headquarters. As things stand, I find myself reluctant to take that trip. I'm afraid to leave my family unprotected."

"I don't know what more I can do — "

"I know enough about policing to know that it's your job to protect a poor, helpless woman like my daughter," Mr. Tyson said.

"If you know anything about policing," Levesque said, "you'll know that I can't arrest people for what they may or may not have done. I need reasonable grounds, not mere suspicion. In this case, that would be someone who actually saw the offence being committed. And you've just told me — "

"It's a sad day," Mr. Tyson said, "when decent law-abiding taxpayers have less influence than convicted criminals. I don't know what it was like in Montreal, Levesque, but I can assure you that in East Hastings, we won't stand for this kind of treatment."

I waited, but all I heard was a car door open and close and a car engine start up. Mr. Tyson, I guessed, heading for home.

I thought about what Levesque had said. If there was a witness, Caleb could be arrested.

I was a witness. I had seen the whole thing. I knew that Caleb had broken the terms of his undertaking. Levesque had let him go on condition that he stay away from Terri. He hadn't lived up to that agreement. If I told Levesque what had happened, Caleb could end up in jail.

But I couldn't make myself tell. The look in Terri's eyes haunted me too much. It wasn't the look of someone who feared or hated the person who had put her in a wheelchair. It was just the opposite — the look of a person crazy in love. And the thing was, Caleb had had the same look on his face.

After a moment, the front door opened. Levesque came in, but he didn't head back to the kitchen where his supper was waiting. Instead he went into the hall closet. When he came out again, he was slipping on his jacket. "I should be home before your mother," he said.

I didn't have to ask where he was going, but I wondered why he was bothering. It was like Mr. Tyson had said — Caleb wasn't likely to confess that he had broken his undertaking.

* * *

That night I heard something that I had never heard before.

I went up to bed around midnight. Levesque still wasn't home, but Mom was. She'd been home for hours.

I must have fallen asleep soon after my head hit the pillow, because I was groggy when I opened my eyes again. I had been awakened by voices. Angry voices. I blinked at the clock on my bedside table. It was a little after one. What was going on?

"That little punk," Levesque said. "I didn't like him when I met him and I like him even less the more I know about him. Why didn't you call me?" His voice rumbled like an avalanche. I had never, ever heard him shout at Mom before. Nor had I ever heard him say that he didn't like someone.

And since when had he never liked Charles Tyson?
"I'd have — "

"You'd have what?" Mom said. "It has nothing to
do with you. It's between me and Charles." Her
voice wasn't nearly as loud as Levesque's, but it
had an edge to it that I recognized. It was the tone
she used when she was asking you to do something
for the hundredth time and you were offering
yet another lame excuse. It was her I'm-tired-of-
saying-this voice. When Mom starts talking in that
tone, you're wise to listen up and to do what she
tells you. "Besides, there's nothing you can do about
it."

"I could have a chat with Charles," Levesque
said. The menace in his voice made me glad that I
wouldn't be on the receiving end of that chat. "In
fact, I think that's exactly what I'll do."

"You will *not*," Mom said. That imperial tone was
another one that Phoebe and I knew well. I wondered if Levesque had encountered it before. "I
don't know why I even told you about it."

"I'm your husband."

"Which means you're my partner," Mom said. "My
equal, not my equalizer. I'm perfectly capable of
handling Charles Tyson on my own. I don't need
the chief of police to run interference for me."

Silence. A long pause. Then murmuring. Then a
giggle. So much for that argument.

* * *

Mom was her usual cheery self at breakfast the
next day. Levesque had already gone to work —

which meant that I had to leave early if I wanted to drop by the police station and beg him for a ride up to Morrisville that afternoon — and I did. I gulped down some coffee, grabbed an orange to eat on the way, shouldered my backpack, hefted the box of first-aid guides and set off down the driveway.

The police station wasn't far from school, so it didn't take me out of my way. I was glad to see that everything was quiet — no angry mobs, no arrests in progress. Just another sleepy Tuesday morning in little old East Hastings.

Levesque was alone in the office. He was sitting at his desk, peering at his computer screen, one hand clicking away with his mouse, the other wrapped around a mug of steaming black coffee. He glanced up at me when I came through the door, then refocused his eyes on the computer screen. "Aren't you supposed to be at school?" he said.

I glanced at the clock on the wall. "Classes don't start for twenty minutes," I said. "Are you super busy this afternoon?"

"Why?" He still wasn't looking at me, which wasn't typical. Usually when I asked him a question — or for a favour — he scrutinized me, looking for the catch or the angle. I was dying to quiz him about why he'd never liked Charles Tyson. But that wasn't the reason I had come, and I didn't dare pose the question. Blatant eavesdropping is frowned upon at my house.

"I'm working on a story for the school paper," I said. "I need to interview kids up in Morrisville."

"Shouldn't you be thinking about getting a driver's license?"

Well, sure. In fact, Get Driver's License was up near the top of my official to-do list. You pretty much need a car up here, unless you're willing to rely on the spotty bus service or beg parents, friends, neighbours, relatives and even relative strangers for a lift whenever you need to go somewhere. "Maybe I can take care of that today," I said. "I mean, I don't have any special plans at lunch."

Now his eyes moved from the screen and zeroed in on me. The look in them was decidedly sour. "What's in the box?"

"First-aid guides. Charles Tyson is donating them to the school."

As soon as I mentioned Tyson's name, the air in the room seemed to chill by ten degrees. Levesque didn't say anything. Nothing at all.

"Please," I said. "I need to do this story."

"The last time I checked, there was bus service between East Hastings and Morrisville."

"The bus is so uncomfortable." It was really just a converted school bus. The company that ran it tried to disguise that fact with a coat of navy blue paint. Tried, but didn't succeed. "And it takes forever."

Levesque's eyes narrowed. "That bus travels at the speed limit," he said. "Are you suggesting that I don't?"

"That bus makes a million stops on the way," I pointed out. Not that there were a million towns between East Hastings and Morrisville. There weren't. There were just a few sleepy hamlets and a lot of farms — and the bus driver was only too happy to pull over and let every farmer's kid or farmer's wife off right at the end of some long farm driveway.

"What time?" he said.

"I can be here at two-thirty."

His eyes narrowed to hairline slits.

"I have last period off to work on the paper," I said. "Geez, I'll bring a note from my teacher if you want."

"That won't be necessary," he said. Then, "I'll see what I can do." Translation: *Police work is unpredictable and always comes first.* "Don't be late." This from a guy who was always issuing don't-wait-supper-for-me alerts.

* * *

Kyle wasn't at school — or if he was, he didn't show up for Mr. Mowat's first-aid class. At first I was relieved. I wouldn't be buddied with him again.

Mr. Mowat held up a copy of the first-aid book we had all received. "I expect you to read this, people," he said. "Cover to cover. There will be a test."

The first-aid lady used Mr. Mowat to demonstrate the CPR technique and then told us to work in teams to practise.

"On your own today, Chloe?" Mr. Mowat said as everyone settled into pairs.

"Yes, sir."

"Well, we can't have that. CPR is something you learn by doing."

I nodded. Whatever. I got up and scanned the twosomes scattered throughout the gym, trying to decide which one I wanted to join. But Mr. Mowat had what he probably considered a better idea.

"Here," he said, dropping down onto his back on the floor at my feet. "You can practise on me."

Funny how time and circumstances can make yesterday's nightmare partner seem like today's dream option. I tried to look on the bright side. I told myself that the day couldn't possibly get any worse.

* * *

I dropped by the newspaper office at lunch to give Ross an update on my story — and to see if he was still mad at me. He wasn't.

"What's the deal with Charles Tyson?" I asked.

"What do you mean?"

"When Caleb arrived back in town, you said that some people behave a certain way when native people are involved — especially Charles. Why especially Charles?"

"Why are you asking?"

I filled him in on what had happened at the Canadian Tire and mentioned that I had heard someone refer to Charles as a punk, but I didn't say who that someone was.

Ross nodded and sighed at the same time. "After high school, Charles went to live in Toronto for a while," he said. "The story I heard is that he was part of a skinhead gang. You should have seen him when he came back here — black leather, shaved head, the whole works. Just like that movie, *American History X.*"

I tried to picture the business-suited store manager I knew in the get-up Ross was describing. "Are you sure we're talking about the same Charles Tyson?" I said.

Ross nodded. "Only he was Charlie then."

"How long ago was that?"

"I don't know," Ross said. "I was just a kid, but I remember seeing him and people talking about him. He came back here about ten years ago, I guess."

"Just about the time Terri started going with Caleb," I said.

"Yeah."

Skinhead Charles comes back to East Hastings to find his sister going out with Caleb Darke. I bet that had gone over big with him.

* * *

Levesque was standing beside his squad car when I arrived at the police station after school.

"You're going to drive me in *that*?" I said. I tried to picture the looks I'd get from the kids up in Morrisville if I was deposited in front of their school in a police cruiser.

"I'm on duty," he said. "It's this or the bus."

I slid into the front passenger seat without another word.

It takes about forty minutes to drive to Morrisville. How long those forty minutes seem depends on who's doing the driving. I've done the trip with Ross talking all the way about his big ideas for the school newspaper — diverting, but not riveting. Time sensation: exactly forty minutes. I've driven it with Rick Antonio, cursing myself all the way for being stupid enough to agree to go out with him. Time sensation: twelve days, and a sickening feeling that the trip was never going to end. I've driven it with Jonah Shackleton, both of us sitting in the back seat of his Aunt Linda's car, talking about this and that. Time sensation: two seconds — and genuine regret that we couldn't ride together forever. When I started out with Levesque, I wasn't sure what to expect. He was quiet. He seemed pre-occupied. What else was new? Time-sensation esti-mate: too long, considering that this was a member of my own family.

We had just left the East Hastings town limits behind when Levesque got a radio call. Steve Den-by. Levesque glanced at me as he took the call. He seemed irked that I was sitting right there, listen-ing to what Steve was saying. He liked to keep a sharp line between police work and family, but it didn't always work out that way.

"It's Caleb Darke," Steve's voice said. "He's caus-ing a disturbance out at Jimmy Johnston's place."

CHAPTER EIGHT

"What kind of disturbance, Steve?" Levesque also seemed irked at having to ask what Steve should have told him straight out in the first place.

"Freddy Deneuve called it in," Steve said. "He wasn't real clear about it. He said 'a disturbance.' Said he thought it might be a good idea if someone went out and calmed things down."

"I can be there in five minutes," Levesque said. "I'll call you if I need backup."

He slowed the car, checked the highway both ways, and then did a U-turn.

"Seatbelt," he said.

I had buckled it as soon as I'd got into the car. "I wasn't born yesterday," I said.

A few seconds later he turned west on a gravel road, going a whole lot faster than the bus to Morrisville could ever have dreamed of going. Going a whole lot faster than the speed limit, too. Not that I was about to point that out.

I had never been to Jimmy Johnston's hunting and fishing camp. I didn't even know where it was. Turns out it isn't hard to find if you can navigate a network of back roads that, as far as I could tell, had as many branches and dead ends as the lines on the average human palm. I got the feeling Levesque could have done it with his eyes closed — although I wouldn't have wanted to be in the car

81

with him if he tried. We barrelled along, spraying gravel from all four tires, before coming to an abrupt stop in a clearing that was flanked on three sides by buildings. One was exactly what I would have imagined a hunting lodge to look like — a two-storey, sprawling wooden structure, roughly but sturdily constructed. The other buildings were smaller. I couldn't tell what they were used for. I didn't spend much time trying to figure it out, either.

There were five people standing outside the lodge. One of them was Caleb. He was holding a big stick in both hands and waving it in front of him, like it was a sword and he was some kind of medieval knight. It seemed to be pretty effective in holding off the two guys who were trying to get at him. A fourth man, one I recognized from the police station and from the Benny's parking lot, was standing back opposite Caleb, rubbing his jaw. Jimmy Johnston. The fifth man, a lot older and a lot smaller than the other four, hurried over to the police car.

Levesque checked his pistol before he opened the driver's-side door. He looked at me and said, "Don't even think about getting out of this car, you hear me?"

I heard.

Levesque got out and closed the car door behind him. When he wasn't looking, I rolled down my window so that I could hear what was going on. "He turned up and said he wanted to talk to the boss," the man was saying. "Things heated up pretty fast after that."

"Anyone hurt, Freddy?"

"Not yet," the man said. "So far both Caleb and Jimmy have held onto their tempers." He sounded surprised,

"Anyone armed?" Levesque said. A logical question, I guess. This was a hunting camp, after all.

Freddy shook his head. "'Cept for that walkin' stick Caleb's got. One of the boys wanted to go for a gun, but I talked 'im out of it."

"Good man," Levesque said.

The muscles in my neck and shoulders tightened up as I watched him walk toward Caleb and the others. Levesque is taller and bulkier than average, but he's just one man. And — although I'm no expert — this seemed to be one of those situations where anything could happen. I don't like guns. The world would be a better place without them. But this was one time when I was glad that Levesque was armed.

Levesque planted himself between Caleb and the other three men. He stood sort of sideways, so he could see everyone.

"You men step back," he said to Jimmy Johnston and the two guys next to him. Then somebody must have said or done something, because one of the men — a tall, wiry guy with mean eyes — suddenly lunged at Caleb. Jimmy and the other man grabbed him and wrenched him back.

"Let the police handle it," Jimmy said. He nodded

to Levesque before taking his men back a few paces.

Levesque turned to Caleb. "How about letting me have that?" he said, holding out his hand for the stick Caleb had been swinging.

Caleb studied him a moment. Maybe it was just my imagination, but he seemed to be having a hard time deciding whether to surrender the stick or use it. Finally, he released his hold on it. Levesque tossed it far into the bushes near one end of the lodge.

"Now, suppose you tell me what's going on here, Caleb?" he said.

"What's going on is he came in here and started threatening the boss," the tall, wiry guy said.

Levesque turned toward Jimmy. "Why don't you take your men inside?" he said. "I'll talk to them after I'm through here."

Jimmy Johnston stood his ground for a few seconds, his eyes drilling into Caleb. Then he nodded to his two men and they all headed into the lodge.

"Freddy, do me a favour," Levesque said to the old guy. "Keep them company. We don't need any more trouble."

"Sure thing," Freddy said. He went inside, leaving Levesque alone with Caleb.

Levesque kept to what I knew was his "interview stance": facing Caleb on an angle, his gun away from him, so that Caleb couldn't grab it. "What seems to be the problem?" he said.

"No problem," Caleb said. He was easily as tall as

Levesque, and had as much bulk. He didn't look at all intimidated.

Levesque stood perfectly still and waited. I knew what that meant. If this were a game show, he'd have said, "Is that your final answer?" It sure wasn't one Levesque was going to accept. "You've been back four days, Caleb, and you're already facing charges. How much harder do you want to make this for yourself?"

Caleb said nothing.

"We can go two ways here," Levesque said. "I can go inside right now and get Johnston's version. Judging from the way he looked, he's going to want to press charges, and based on what I saw when I came in here, I'm going to have to go along with that. *Or*" — he paused a moment to let that little word sink in — "you can give me your side of the story first. Give me something to go on, so I can see if I can't calm this thing down a little and keep you out of more trouble. Your choice, Caleb."

"I used to work here sometimes," Caleb said finally. "Back before Terri and I were together." He glanced up at the lodge, then back at Levesque. "Terri worked here too, that year." He didn't say which year, but Levesque nodded as if he already knew. "I was just dropping by, you know, just saying hello, that's all."

Maybe he hadn't seen Jimmy at the bus stop. Maybe he hadn't known how Jimmy felt about him being back. So maybe that explained why he was here at Jimmy's lodge. But it didn't explain the stick he'd been swinging. Levesque must have felt the same way, because he stood there, quiet, staring hard at Caleb, still waiting.

Caleb drew in a deep breath before continuing. "Pip came after me," he said. "He told me if I didn't get off the property, he was going to make me." I guessed Pip was the tall, wiry guy. "It had nothing to do with him. I came to talk to Mr. Johnston." Not Jimmy, I noticed, but *Mr. Johnston*.

Levesque studied Caleb a little more closely. "I'm going to put you in the car, Caleb," he said. "And I'm going to expect you to behave yourself while I go and talk to Johnston. You got that?"

Caleb nodded. He and Levesque started toward me. Levesque opened the back door. I faced resolutely forward while Caleb got in.

"I mean it, Caleb," Levesque said. "Don't give me a reason to go any harder on you than I have to," he said. "And Chloe? You don't move from there, you hear?"

Yeah, I heard.

Levesque shut the back door of the patrol car. I watched him turn, walk up to the lodge and go inside.

The little hairs on the back of my neck stood smartly at attention when I realized I was alone — completely alone — with Caleb. Up close, he was big. Really big. There was an energy coming off him, a restlessness, maybe from being locked up for so long. He shifted in the back seat and I reminded myself that there was a secure partition between him and me. Then I felt ashamed of myself for thinking that. I pride myself on being a fair-minded person. I don't always live up to this ideal, but I do try.

The truth is, though, that I was a little on edge. I was sitting alone in a car with a guy who had either beaten his girlfriend almost to death and left her life in ruins, or who had served eight years for a crime he hadn't committed. Either way, he was not the happiest and most well-adjusted of people. If he really had done it, then he was a guy with a violent past who'd been making all the wrong moves since he got back to town. If he hadn't done it, then he was probably angry and bitter for having spent eight years of his life behind bars — and maybe that accounted for his reckless actions these past few days.

I glanced into the rearview mirror. Caleb was staring right back at me. I turned to look at him, mostly to show him that I wasn't afraid — even if I wasn't entirely sure that was true. I even smiled at him. He didn't smile back. He didn't even really look at me. Instead, he seemed to be looking through me.

Well, okay. I turned around again, dug in my backpack and pulled out my first-aid manual. I opened it and flipped through the pages on shock and wounds. Ooh, lookee here, how to deal with stab wounds and gunshot wounds — as if I would ever encounter anything like that! I was so focused on the book that I wasn't paying any attention to what was going on outside. Then, *bang!*

It took a moment — no, a split second — for the source of the sound to register. Caleb had turned in the back seat and hammered both of his fists against the window. My heart thudded to a stop in my chest. *Bang!* His fists hammered the window again.

That did it.

My hand clamped down on the door handle. I shoved the door open and scrambled out onto the hard-packed earth. Once I was safely outside, I turned to look back at the car. Caleb was staring out the window with those black eyes of his. He wasn't looking at me, though. He was staring at Charles Tyson, who was climbing out of his car. Charles looked over at Caleb, locked in the back of the police car. Looked and smiled, before circling his car and opening the trunk. He started to unload some boxes.

"Chloe!" Levesque's voice. I turned toward it, relief flooding over me as he came out of the lodge, looking not very pleased.

"I thought I told you to wait in the car," he said.

"I needed some air."

He peered hard at me — trying to read me, I guess. Then he glanced at Charles and followed Charles's gaze. "Stay right here," Levesque said to me. "Don't move. You think you can do that?"

"What am I?" I said. "A dog? Sit, Chloe. Stay, Chloe."

Levesque just shook his head. Okay, bad analogy.

Even Shendor is more obedient than I am.

I stayed put while Levesque had a word with Charles. Then he opened the back door of the patrol car and leaned down to talk to Caleb. He kept his voice low, so this time I couldn't hear what he was saying. When he shut the door again, he beckoned me back into the car.

"We're driving Caleb home," he said. "Then I'll run you up to Morrisville."

That answered one of my questions: Caleb obviously wasn't under arrest. Maybe another question would soon be answered: How come Kyle hadn't shown up in class today?

* * *

Levesque checked in with Steve to let him know that everything was under control. Apart from that, we drove mostly in silence.

Caleb lived even deeper in the bush than Jimmy Johnston. Levesque had to slow the squad car down to a crawl for the last half kilometre or so. The gravel road was grooved and rutted and, in a few places, partly collapsed. Finally, we pulled into a small clearing. In the middle of the clearing sat a sad, sagging house. A rusting pickup truck was parked in front. Around one side I saw a battered green car that looked older than me. As Levesque killed the squad car's engine, the cabin door opened and Thaddeus Darke came out. Immediately behind him was Kyle.

Levesque glanced at me. A look really can say it all. This one said, Stay! He got out, circled the car and opened the back door. Caleb went straight into the house.

Levesque stood outside for a few minutes, talking to Thaddeus Darke. Kyle hung back a few paces, listening, I guess. That's what I would have done if my brother had been brought home in the back of a police car. He glanced at me a couple of times, but didn't smile or give any sign that he knew me, let alone that he'd consider talking to me. Nice.

Levesque got back into the car and we bounced down the gravel road again. For a while I didn't say anything. Finally, though, I couldn't stand it.

"Why didn't you arrest him?" I said.

"For what?"

"For waving that big stick around." I didn't know what the official charge for that would be, but I was pretty sure there had to be some kind of law that covered the situation.

Levesque stared straight ahead, concentrating so hard on his driving that you'd have thought he was guiding the car through a minefield. I'd assumed he was going to do what he usually did when I stuck my nose into police business — pretend he hadn't heard my question. But he surprised me.

"Caleb said he went there to talk to Jimmy Johnston. He said that when Johnston told him to leave, one of Johnston's men provoked him. Johnston told the same story — he said he didn't want to press charges."

I worked that one through. I had seen Jimmy Johnston outside the police station the day before

Caleb arrived back in town. He had looked as angry as the two Tysons. He had also been part of the get-out-of-town crowd the next day, when the bus had pulled into Benny's.

"Why would he say that?" I said. "He doesn't seem to like Caleb any better than the Tyson family does."

Levesque didn't answer that. Instead he said, "It's a good thing Freddy was there and called it in before things got out of hand."

"What was Charles doing there?" I said.

"Making a delivery."

I shook my head. He wouldn't deliver first-aid manuals to my school, which was a couple of blocks from his store, but he'd drive all the way out here? He and Jimmy Johnston must be good friends.

When we reached the highway, Levesque glanced at me. "Which way?"

I checked my watch. It was three forty-five. It would be four-thirty by the time we got to Morrisville. There would be hardly anyone left at school. Another day lost on my story.

"Home, I guess," I said. "Maybe I'll take the bus up there tomorrow."

* * *

"I'll get it done," I told Ross again the next day and — if I knew Ross — not for the last time, either. Ross could out-nag any mother any time.

"When?" he said. "You were supposed to go up there yesterday to do some interviews. Now you tell me, oops, you didn't get there?"

At lunch I had steered clear of the newspaper office and the cafeteria — in fact, the whole school — precisely because I hadn't wanted to run into Ross. I hadn't wanted to explain that my trip to Morrisville had been derailed, and I hadn't wanted to be subjected to his world-class badgering. I'd decided to head up to Centre Street, instead, and maybe grab a slice of pizza. It was just my luck to run into Ross in the school parking lot. He tagged along with me, walking backwards mostly — the better to harangue me about deadlines and journalistic responsibilities, blah blah blah.

"I didn't, *oops*, not get there," I said. "I was with Levesque and he had to take a call and by the time everything got sorted out, it was too late. It wasn't my fault."

"I don't want to end up with a big blank spot on page eleven," he said.

Wait a minute! "Page *eleven*? You're driving me crazy about a story that you're going to bury on page eleven? Geez, if you get stuck, you can always run an ad for the yearbook." *Or something equally boring.* "And how come I get all the stupid assignments? What are *you* working on, Ross?"

I knew from the hand-in-the-cookie-jar look on his face that he hadn't assigned himself anything nearly as lame as he'd handed me.

"What, Ross?"

He stared at the toes of his sneakers as if they held the secret of the universe. "I'm doing a piece on capital punishment," he said at last.

"Why? Is someone planning drastic action against a certain annoying newspaper editor?"

He at least had the decency to look embarrassed. "It's one of the issues that gets discussed in law class, and now there's a Canadian about to be executed in Texas."

"James Walter?"

He nodded. I'd read about the case. It was a good idea for an article. I wished I'd thought of it. We talked about it, and the newspaper in general. Then — maybe it was something in my voice, or maybe it was something in my face — Ross stopped nattering about deadlines and turned to look where I was looking.

Which meant that we both saw it. We both saw my sister Phoebe standing with Kyle Darke in front of Lawrence Furniture and Appliances, which is right next to Frank's Sports Bar. Frank was having the sidewalk outside his place made into an outdoor patio. We both saw Kyle pick up a large interlocking paving brick from the pile waiting to be turned into Frank's patio. We both saw Phoebe say something to him. We both saw the expression on her face change from surprise to alarm as Kyle raised the paving brick above his head. We both saw Phoebe move toward him, her arms outstretched.

And we both saw Kyle sidestep her and heave the paving brick through the plate-glass window of Lawrence Furniture and Appliances.

CHAPTER NINE

"Geez," Ross said as the front window of Lawrence's shattered. He pulled a reporter's notebook from his pocket.

"What is it with those Darkes?" I said.

"What is it with your sister?" Ross said.

About a nanosecond after the brick had shattered the front window of the store, a plump, red-faced man raced out onto the sidewalk, yelling. He grabbed Kyle by the collar of his T-shirt and held him fast. The man was a good half-foot shorter than Kyle, and several decades older. Kyle could have shaken him off easily — not that it would have done him much good. He had been seen and could be identified. He didn't even try to break free. He just stood there, holding his head high for a change instead of looking down at the ground. Phoebe was saying something to the man, who didn't seem to be paying any attention.

"Geez," Ross said again.

The man who had Kyle by the collar was gesturing with one hand. A few moments later, a younger man came out of the store and said something to Phoebe.

I started to cross the street.

"Hey!" Ross started to say. "Don't you think we should just — "

I didn't stick around to hear the rest.

"Phoebe," I said, grabbing her by the arm. She was still trying to talk to the plump man.

"He didn't mean it, Mr. Lawrence," she said two or three times. *Nice try, Pheebs,* I thought. *A guy picks up a paving brick, resists all efforts to make him put it down and instead throws it through a window, and he didn't mean it?*

"Phoebe, what's going on?"

She looked startled to see me. Then her eyes widened even more, and I turned to see Levesque and Steve Denby striding down the street toward the store. Phoebe gulped. She really did. I heard the little *urp* sound in her throat.

Levesque zeroed in on me. Not Phoebe, *me* — as if, of course, if there was trouble in town, my presence was a given.

"I was just passing by with Ross," I said, gesturing toward intrepid reporter Ross Jenkins, who was still safely on the other side of the street. "If you want to know what's going on, ask Phoebe."

Levesque glanced at Phoebe before turning to Mr. Lawrence. "What seems to be the problem?" he said.

Mr. Lawrence spluttered out his understanding of what had gone on, which boiled down to this: he was standing at the cash register on the other side of the glass, checking the morning's accounts, when something came flying through his front window and landed with a thud at his feet. "Narrowly missing them," he said, his voice shrill. "Then I came out here and grabbed this boy here," he said. He was still hanging onto Kyle's collar.

"You can release him to me, Mr. Lawrence," Levesque said.

Mr. Lawrence looked dubious, but he released his grip on Kyle. Levesque sent Steve inside with Mr. Lawrence to look at the damage and take a statement. Then he turned to Kyle.

"You're going to have to come with me, son," he said. Kyle held himself tall, which I still couldn't figure out. Usually he walked around hunched over, staring at the toes of his sneakers. Levesque looked at Phoebe. "You're here because . . . ?"

"She's with me," Kyle said, and he took Phoebe's hand into his.

I almost fell over. It was the first time I had heard Kyle speak up. And not only was he standing tall for a change, he was holding my sister's hand. Proudly. But why? What had pushed him?

"And you?" Levesque said to me.

"I'm a witness," I said. "I saw the whole thing."

"Terrific," Levesque said, in a voice that made it clear he considered the situation to be many things, but terrific wasn't one of them. "In that case, you can all come with me."

We marched down the street to the police station. Levesque made Phoebe and me sit on a bench near one wall while he took Kyle to his desk and sat him down. He said something to Kyle and handed him the telephone. Kyle started punching in numbers. After he had spoken into the phone, he handed the receiver to Levesque, who spoke to whoever was on the other end of the line. I guessed it was Kyle's uncle.

Then Levesque took Kyle into another room — the room where he interviewed people — and closed the door, leaving Phoebe and me alone in the outer office. We both knew better than to move.

"What happened?" I asked Phoebe.

"Caleb had a job set up at Lawrence's before he moved back here. He started working there Monday morning. But this morning Mr. Lawrence told him he had to let him go. He said there wasn't enough work for Caleb. Kyle doesn't think that's true. He says people just want Caleb gone. He says it's not fair, that Caleb served his time."

"So he smashed the front window in broad daylight, in front of witnesses?" I said. "Smart."

"He was angry."

"What he did was wrong."

Phoebe looked close to tears. "What do you think is going to happen?"

I shrugged. "He'll be charged with something, for sure." I sighed and looked at the door to the interview room. "Why does Kyle think Mr. Lawrence was lying?"

Phoebe was staring at the closed door too. I wondered how close she and Kyle were.

"Caleb told Kyle that Daniel Tyson came into the store yesterday. He and Mr. Lawrence went into Mr. Lawrence's office and shut the door. Caleb said they were in there for a long time and when they came out, Mr. Lawrence didn't look happy. He gave

Caleb a funny look. At least, that's what Caleb told Kyle. Then this morning, like I said, Mr. Lawrence phoned Caleb and told him that he was sorry, but he had to let him go."

I had to admit, it sounded like more than coincidence.

Levesque came out of the interview room. Kyle wasn't with him. Kyle was underage, which meant that Levesque had to wait until Kyle had his uncle or some other adult with him before he could be questioned. While Levesque waited, the door to the police station opened and Steve Denby came in. He went straight over to Levesque and the two of them conferred. Levesque nodded. He didn't look pleased at whatever Steve was telling him.

"You stay here and wait for Thaddeus Darke," Levesque told him.

He glanced over at us. He opened his desk drawer and pulled out two pads of paper and two pens. He crooked a finger at Phoebe. She got up. He handed her one of the pads and one of the pens and directed her to his desk. Then he handed me the second pad and pen and told me to stay put. "Write down exactly what you saw," he told us. "Put the date at the top of the page and sign it when you're finished. If you write more than one page, sign each one. No talking, just writing. When you're done, give the pads back to Steve and go back to school. Got it?"

We nodded in unison.

I glanced at Phoebe, who did not look happy. She

bowed her head, but didn't start writing right away. I looked up at Levesque.

"Write," he said. Then, "Keep an eye on these two, Steve. I'll be back in a few minutes."

I sighed and started to write down exactly what I had seen. It took Phoebe longer to get started. I wondered how truthful she was being. When I had finished and saw that Phoebe was still writing, I stopped and re-read my page and a half.

"Finished, Chloe?" Steve asked.

"In a minute," I said, and snuck another peek at Phoebe. She was still writing.

The door to the police station opened and Thaddeus Darke stepped in. "You have my nephew," he said to Steve.

Steve nodded. "He's in the interview room, Mr. Darke," he said. "You can see him if you'd like. The chief will be back soon. He'll have some questions for Kyle."

Mr. Darke didn't ask what Kyle was doing at the police station. He didn't ask what kind of questions Levesque would have. He just nodded and headed for the door that Steve had indicated.

Phoebe put down her pen.

"Finished?" Steve said.

She nodded glumly, as if what she had just finished doing was knotting a noose around Kyle's neck, which meant that whatever she had written, it was the truth. She got up and handed her pad of paper to Steve. So did I. We left the police station together. Once we were outside, though, neither of us was in any hurry to get back to school.

Then we heard a whistle. A long, shrill trill. From across the street, Ross beckoned.

"Come on," I said to Phoebe.

She looked back at the police station.

"*Come on*," I said again. "If Levesque comes back and finds us hanging around here instead of heading back to school, he won't be happy." What an understatement. I grabbed her by the arm and dragged her across the street with me.

Ross was twitching all over, which was how I knew he had something he was desperate to tell us. I was right.

"I talked to Howie Eccles," he said.

I'd never heard the name before. The gleam of excitement on Ross's face made it clear that if I wanted to know more, I was going to have to ask. All right, then. "And Howie Eccles is . . . ?"

"He graduated high school last year. He works at Lawrence's now." Ross glanced up and down the street, then dropped his voice lower. "He told me that Daniel Tyson pressured Mr. Lawrence into letting Caleb go. Mr. Lawrence didn't want to do it."

"See?" Phoebe said triumphantly. "Didn't I tell you?"

"If Mr. Lawrence didn't want to let Caleb go, why didn't he stand up to Mr. Tyson?" I asked.

"Mr. Lawrence has a loan application in at the bank that Mr. Tyson manages. Mr. Tyson also has a lot of influence in town. He can make life hard for Mr. Lawrence if he wants to."

"But that's practically blackmail," Phoebe said.

"It *is* blackmail," I said. "Daniel Tyson wants to get Caleb out of town. What better way than to make sure he can't get work here?"

"We have to do something," Phoebe said. Tears of rage glistened in the corners of her eyes. "We have to tell Dad."

"I think he already knows," Ross said. "He was talking to Mr. Lawrence when I was talking to Howie."

"And?"

"And why don't you ask him?" Ross said. He nodded toward the street. I turned and saw Levesque heading back to the police station.

"Come on," I said, grabbing Ross and Phoebe. Levesque had ordered us to school. Time to go.

We got back just as the bell for fourth period rang. When Ross heard it, he turned pale and sprinted across the parking lot, as if he were being pursued by a posse of hall monitors. Ross has built his whole high-school career around following the rules. Rule number one at East Hastings Regional: *Be on time — or else.*

Phoebe also has a reputation for punctuality. But she turned away from me listlessly and headed for the door like a soon-to-be-dead man walking a pirate's plank. I caught her by the arm.

"What's going on with you and Kyle?" I said.

She shrugged. "I don't know." She sounded sincere enough. "I like him. I think he likes me too."

I thought about him catching her hand in his and

telling Levesque proudly, *She's with me.*

"I think so too. And Phoebe? I think it's good. I think he could use a friend."

She nodded. She didn't walk into school any faster, but she did walk a little taller.

* * *

By the end of the school day, everyone was talking about what Kyle had done. Most people said they weren't surprised. After all, look at what Caleb had done. Kyle was just taking after his big brother. I could only imagine what they were thinking and saying in the Tyson household.

Levesque came home for supper, but only picked at his food. When Phoebe asked him if what Ross had said was true — that Mr. Tyson had pressured Mr. Lawrence into dismissing Caleb — Levesque grunted irritably, but didn't deny it.

"Kyle says you didn't charge him," she said.

Levesque sighed and poked at the pork chop on his plate. "You can thank Mr. Lawrence for that. He finally agreed to drop the charges if Kyle promised to pay for the damage."

I tried to imagine Kyle agreeing to these terms. "And Kyle promised?" I said.

"His uncle paid for the window. As I understand it, Kyle will be forgoing his allowance for the foreseeable future."

Phoebe stared down at her plate for a few moments. When she finally raised her head again, she looked directly at Levesque and said, "Did you know that Charles Tyson killed Kyle's grandfather?"

"*What?*" I said. Talk about a bombshell!

Levesque sat perfectly still. Even before he opened his mouth, that solid pose told me his answer to Phoebe's question. He knew. He had probably known before Caleb even got off the bus at Benny's — before the rest of us around the table had even heard of Caleb Darke. "That was an accident," Levesque said.

I remembered the headstone in the cemetery. "Are we talking about Matthew Sunday?" I asked.

Phoebe nodded. "Charles Tyson shot him."

"My goodness," Mom said. "Those two families are like the Capulets and Montagues."

Romeo and Juliet. Ross had said the same thing. He'd also told me that Caleb had once beaten up Charles Tyson. No wonder.

"And the shooting was an accident?" I said.

"A hunting accident," Levesque said. "It happens up here sometimes. Not often, but it happens."

"But wasn't Kyle's father *also* killed in a hunting accident?" I said.

Phoebe nodded. "Two months before Kyle was born. Then his mother died, and his grandfather looked after him and Caleb until . . . " Her voice trailed off.

Levesque looked at her for a few moments, the way you'd look at someone you hadn't seen in a few years — that quick couple of seconds when you tried to figure out exactly what was different about the person. "I don't know if that boy will listen to you or not," he said, "but you might want to tell him that there are better ways to make a point than to engage in criminal activity."

Phoebe lowered her eyes and didn't look up again until Levesque shoved his plate aside — he had hardly touched his food — and announced that he was going back to the office. The phone rang as he was getting to his feet. He disappeared into the kitchen. When he came back, he told Mom not to wait up for him.

"Problem?" she said.

"Trouble at Jimmy Johnston's place," Levesque said, his face grim.

I couldn't help wondering if the person who had caused the trouble was Caleb Darke.

CHAPTER TEN

I am not normally a morning person. In fact, my idea of heaven would be to stay in bed until at least noon every day — or even until one or two in the afternoon — then to get up and stay up all night. I don't know why. There's just something about the stillness of the night that appeals to me. But having the soul of an owl doesn't mean that I can't haul myself out of bed at the crack of dawn when the situation demands it. And the situation demanded it if I wanted to get the inside story on the trouble at Jimmy Johnston's. Or, at least, try to get the inside story.

"Morning," I said to Levesque. He was in the kitchen, drinking a cup of coffee and reading the city newspaper that was delivered to our door every morning.

"Morning," he said, without looking up from his paper. Actually, it sounded more like a grunt.

I got a mug from the cupboard and reached past him for the coffee pot. "So, how's Mr. Johnston?" I said.

Levesque's eyes came up from the paper. He gave me a look that told me he knew exactly what I was doing. "He's fine. There was no serious damage."

"To him or to his place?"

"Chloe . . . " It never ceased to amaze me how he could make my name sound like a warning and a threat, all at the same time. I don't think that's what Mom had in mind when she chose it for me.

"Come on," I said. "Like Mr. Torelli isn't going to run the whole story in the next issue of the *Beacon*."

"Then you can read about it there, same as everyone else," Levesque said.

I shook my head as I sipped my coffee. "I don't understand why Caleb would do something that stupid," I said. "The way I heard it, he spent all that time in prison denying that he'd hurt Terri. But all he's done since he got back is get into trouble."

Levesque likes to play it cool. He likes to keep his face neutral. He likes to think he can't be read. Most of the time, he's right. But he has a little flaw that's a dead giveaway. He gets annoyed when people jump to stupid conclusions that are hurtful to people — people who are presumed to be innocent until proven guilty. And when he gets annoyed his coal-black eyes zero in on whoever he's annoyed with and hold that person — in this case, me — until they're ready to start babbling an apology, which I refused to do. I hadn't said anything even remotely inaccurate.

"You're not going to tell me that Mr. Johnston didn't tell you it was Caleb who did it," I said, knowing perfectly well that he wasn't going to tell me anything at all.

Sure enough, I got no answer. Levesque set his empty mug in the sink, abandoned his newspaper on the kitchen counter and left the room. I heard the front door open and then close again. Then

Mom came into the kitchen.

"When did Phoebe leave?" she asked.

I didn't even know she was gone.

* * *

I had decided to walk by the police station on my way to school. I hadn't really expected to see anything, but for once life exceeded my expectations. When I was still a block away, I saw an old rust bucket of a pickup truck pull up across the street. Both doors opened. Thaddeus Darke stepped out onto the street. Kyle stepped onto the sidewalk.

Then someone else got out: Phoebe.

Thaddeus and Kyle Darke went into the police station. I called to Phoebe, but she had already disappeared around a corner.

* * *

"Kyle is alibiing Caleb," Ross said when I ran into him in the hall before school. "There's no way your dad's going to buy that."

"How do you know that?"

"Well, he strikes me as a sensible person, and if it were me, I wouldn't believe a guy's brother — "

"No," I said. "I mean, how do you know that Kyle is alibiing Caleb?" I also wanted to ask, *alibiing him for what?* But I didn't want to admit to Ross how little I knew.

A half smile flickered across Ross's lips. He seemed to think I was kidding.

"*Everyone* knows," he said. "I also heard he stole some guns from Mr. Johnston."

"Guns?"

"Hunting rifles," Ross said. "Geez, Chloe, everyone's talking about it."

Everyone except the top cop's step-daughter. I asked Ross to fill me in, which he was irritatingly delighted to do, after he sketched out his personal grapevine for me.

"We live next door to Freddy Deneuve's sister," he said. "She and my mom went to school together. They're practically best friends."

Freddy Deneuve? The only Freddy I knew was . . . of course. The guy who worked for Jimmy Johnston.

"Freddy told his sister that Jimmy Johnston was alone at his place last night, when he noticed that the door to his gun room was unlocked — "

"Gun room?"

"Where he keeps his hunting rifles. You're supposed to keep them locked up," Ross said.

Okay.

"He noticed the room was unlocked and when he went inside, someone attacked him with a knife. He said the guy who attacked him was Caleb Darke."

"Was he badly hurt?"

"He had to have stitches," Ross said. "I think Freddy said he was stabbed in his left arm."

"What else did Freddy say?"

"Freddy and Thaddeus Darke are friendly — always have been, even with what happened with Caleb. Freddy said that when your dad went to the Darke place to find Caleb, he wasn't there, and neither his uncle nor Kyle knew where he was. But Kyle claims that he and Caleb were together at the time Mr. Johnston says he was attacked. Of course, nobody believes Kyle."

"Why *of course*?"

Ross gave me a look that said, *Are you running a fever or something?* "If I said that Phoebe had attacked me and you said she'd been with you at the time and couldn't have done it, do you think anyone would believe you?" he said.

"What if I was the one who was telling the truth and you were the one who was lying?" I said.

"Why would I *lie*?" Ross said indignantly.

Good question. "Maybe for the same reason Daniel Tyson pressured Mr. Lawrence into letting Caleb go. To get him out of town and away from Terri." Terri, who had looked so happy to see Caleb.

Everyone at school was talking about what had happened. Nobody believed that Kyle was telling the truth when he said he'd been with Caleb at the time.

Well, almost nobody. I was headed down the second-floor hallway on my way to French class when I heard something that sounded like a slap, followed by something that was definitely a yelp. I turned and saw Phoebe scowling at Jenny Fillion, who, until that moment, I had thought was Phoebe's best friend. Jenny was holding a hand over one cheek. She looked stupefied.

Ms Pileggi, one of the math teachers, must have been attracted by the same two noises. She was advancing on Phoebe. By the time I'd reached the scene of the crime, Phoebe was being dispatched to the office.

I headed down the hall with her. "What was that all about?" I asked, as if I couldn't guess.

"Kyle is not lying," she said, her voice trembling. "If he said he was with Caleb, then he was with Caleb."

"Is that what he told you this morning?"

She glowered at me. "I believe him," she said fiercely.

We rounded the corner and saw Mr. Moore waiting at the door to the office. Ms Pileggi must have called down to him. His arms were crossed over his chest and he fixed us with a stern look.

I squeezed Phoebe's arm. "He's not as bad as he seems," I said. After all, he had passed on suspending me for the fight in the schoolyard. "Tell him exactly what happened. And if there's the slightest chance that you're sorry for slapping Jenny, tell him that, too."

Phoebe looked at me as if I had suggested she swallow a live rattlesnake. Too bad, because vice-principals love contrition almost as much as they like handing out detentions. As I watched her walk the last few steps to the office as if she were walking that last long mile, I decided that things between her and Kyle had to be serious. They were turning my brown-noser sister into the school bad girl.

* * *

I was sprawled on the couch late that afternoon, plowing through my history textbook, when the front door opened and Mom, Levesque and Phoebe all came in together. Mom looked upset, Levesque looked tense and Phoebe looked like she had been crying. She ran up to her room and slammed the door. Mom sighed and went up after her. Levesque headed for the kitchen. He was pulling a container of milk out of the fridge when I got there.

"What's with Phoebe?" I asked innocently.

"Trouble at school," he said.

"Serious?"

"Nothing that can't be dealt with." He gulped some milk.

"So, did you find Caleb yet?" I asked, and was pleased that this managed to elicit a look of surprise. "The upside of living in a small town," I said. "Or the downside, depending on how you look at it. News travels fast."

"If only it would travel accurately," he said.

"So, did you find him?"

Levesque shook his head. He swallowed the rest of his milk and put the container back into the fridge just as Mom came into the kitchen.

"I've never seen her so upset," she said. "Do you think Kyle is lying, Louis?"

"Maybe," he said. "Maybe not." He blew out an exasperated sigh. "I don't have enough information to go on."

That was interesting. If he didn't have enough information to decide whether or not Kyle was lying, that also meant that he didn't have enough information to decide whether or not Jimmy Johnston was telling the truth. Both stories couldn't be true.

Mom slipped an arm around his waist. "Worried

about that meeting tonight?" she said.

"What meeting?" I said.

"The mayor has called a special meeting," Mom said. "A lot of people have been expressing . . . *concerns* about Caleb Darke. They want a chance to talk about their concerns."

I glanced at Levesque. He looked less than thrilled at the prospect of hearing what the concerned citizens of East Hastings had to say.

"I'd better get supper going," Mom said. "You don't want to face something like that on an empty stomach."

I volunteered to help.

* * *

Supper was more fun than a funeral, but just barely. Phoebe stared down at her plate the whole time and hardly ate a bite. Levesque opened his mouth only to shovel food into it. Mom made a few attempts to start a conversation, and I tried to help her keep it going, but it was like trying to kindle a fire with twigs and a water-soaked match.

"Phoebe and I will clean up," I told Mom.

When I said *Phoebe and I*, I meant we'd make it a team effort, as in two people working together toward a common goal. But Phoebe hung up her dishtowel as soon as she heard the gravel crunching under the tires of Levesque's car.

"Hey!" I said. "You're not finished yet."

"Yes, I am," she said.

I followed her out of the kitchen, dripping soapy, greasy dishwater onto the floor. "If you think I'm going to dry those pots for you — "

"Let them dry in the rack," she said. "I'm going to that meeting. I want to hear what those people say."

Well, that made one of us. I had heard all the opinions I cared to about Caleb Darke.

"You owe me one," I called from the door. But by then she was halfway down the driveway. She didn't answer.

I went back into the kitchen to finish washing — and drying — everything that wouldn't go into the dishwasher. I was wiping down the kitchen counter when Shendor started barking and scratching at the back door.

"Forget it," I said. "You were just out." I grabbed her by the collar and tugged her away from the door. "Now lie down," I said. "And be quiet." I spoke the words firmly, the way Mom always does, and closed a hand over her muzzle to reinforce the message. Shendor responded by being silent — for all of two seconds, exactly the time it took me to pull my hand away. Then she shot over to the back door again. For some reason, she seemed desperate to get out. Well, fine. She was a big dog. She knew her way around the yard. And she'd probably be quieter out there than she was in here.

I opened the back door.

Actually, I started to open it. Shendor shoved her nose into the gap and bumped the door wide open. Then she was off, nails — which obviously needed clipping — skittering across the wooden porch. She reached the steps, launched herself into the air and sailed out into the yard, barking the whole time. A moment later she disappeared into the trees at the end of our property and almost instantly fell silent.

I stood up on the porch, waiting for her to reappear.

She didn't.

I opened my mouth to call her but, in the end, said nothing. I don't know exactly why, but a feeling had stolen over me. A feeling that something was wrong. Shendor barking — that was irritatingly normal. So was her habit of rocketing out of the house when given half a chance — even half a centimetre. But this abrupt silence — this was not normal.

I crept down the steps and headed for the trees. The silence started to spook me.

I came to a stop about a metre from where the trees began, frozen by the pair of black eyes that were staring at me. Caleb Darke was kneeling on the ground, scratching Shendor's ears and talking softly to her. Her tail was whisking back and forth. She looked at me with pleasure-glazed eyes. She was in doggie heaven.

Caleb stood up when I stopped walking. My heart pounded in my chest. I looked at Caleb's hands — they were huge, with spidery long fingers — and remembered what he had supposedly done to Terri. Beat her up and left her for dead — that's what everyone said. Well, everyone except Eric.

Then another picture came into my mind: how tenderly his hand had covered Terri's, and the look of bliss in Terri's eyes. I remembered what Eric had said — that Caleb could have got out of prison sooner if he had accepted responsibility for attacking Terri, but he had refused to do it. Refused because he insisted he had never hurt her.

I called Shendor to me. She left Caleb only reluctantly and came to stand beside me. I put a hand on her head. The warmth of it made me feel a little safer, which I knew was illogical. Shendor was too much of a pushover to be a guard dog. She would have traded my life for a scratch behind the ears any time of day, any day of the week.

"Is he home?" Caleb said. His voice was as quiet as Kyle's.

I shook my head. "He's at a meeting in town."

Caleb looked up at the house, like maybe he didn't believe me. Maybe he thought he'd spot Levesque in a window. When he looked back at me, his eyes were blank, impossible to read.

"Tell him I didn't do it," he said. "Tell him no one is going to make me go away. No one is going to stop me from being with her." He took a step toward me. Automatically, I retreated a pace. "Tell him, okay?"

I nodded.

He held my eyes for a moment before bending down to scratch behind Shendor's ears one last time. Then he turned and loped away. A moment later, he had vanished among the trees.

I sank down to the ground and wrapped my arms around Shendor's neck.

CHAPTER ELEVEN

I headed for the municipal building to find Levesque. As I made my way inside, I wondered how the meeting was going. I had my answer as soon as I opened the door to the auditorium — not well.

The room was packed with angry people. Levesque and the mayor were sitting at a table up front. Two microphones had been set up on either side of the room. Lines of people snaked out behind each one. Charles Tyson was speaking into one of the microphones.

"What's more important to this town?" he was saying in a loud, sharp voice. "Decent, law-abiding taxpayers or convicted felons?" The crowd rumbled around him. "I've lived here most of my life. I run a business in this town that employs people who live here and are raising families here. I pay my taxes, just like all of you. And yet I find myself fearing for my sister's life. That's right. For her *life*. And why? Because the man who brutally attacked her is back among us. He broke into my parents' house. He attacked a good friend of my family."

I glanced at Levesque, who was staring, stone-faced, at Charles Tyson. I thought about what he had said to Mom: *I don't have enough information to go on.*

"And what have the police done about this?" Charles said. "I'll tell you what — nothing. I have two questions. The first is for the mayor and the second for the chief of police. First, what is the mayor doing to make sure that the protection of innocent citizens is a top priority in this town? Second, what is the chief of police doing to rid this town of convicted felons like Caleb Darke?"

All around me, people shouted their support for Charles's questions. They all wanted answers.

The mayor stood up and assured everyone that the citizens of East Hastings were his only priority and that he would do everything he could to make sure that they felt safe and secure. He didn't explain his plan, though. Instead, he looked at Levesque and said, "Perhaps you can elaborate on what action you have taken to date, Chief."

Levesque leaned toward the microphone in front of him. He didn't shout, the way Charles Tyson had. He spoke slowly, deliberately, calmly. "The East Hastings police department is doing the same thing it always does: making sure that anyone caught breaking the law is apprehended and dealt with," he said. "We want everyone to feel safe — "

"Does Jimmy Johnston feel safe?" someone yelled.

"What about Terri Tyson?" someone else yelled.

"Why hasn't Caleb Darke been arrested for stabbing Jimmy Johnston?" Charles Tyson shouted into his microphone.

"We're investigating that incident," Levesque said evenly. Anyone who didn't know him well would think his temper was under perfect control.

Anyone who lived in the same house as him could see that he had just gone from a slow simmer to a rolling boil.

"What's to investigate?" Charles Tyson said. "Jimmy Johnston identified his attacker. Why isn't Caleb Darke in custody? Why hasn't he been charged with attempted murder?"

Suddenly everyone was yelling. Well, almost everyone. In the middle of all the mayhem, I saw an elderly woman, seated, frowning but not angry. If anything, she looked thoughtful. She also looked vaguely familiar. Then I remembered — I had seen her in the parking lot the day Caleb Darke had returned to town. She had been at the very fringes of the crowd that day, watching rather than shouting, curious rather than outraged.

With few exceptions, the crowd surged up out of the auditorium seats. The mayor leapt up and waved his arms, begging for calm. He didn't get it. I saw my mother up near the front of the room. She was trying to edge closer to Levesque, but people swirled around her, separating them.

Finally, Levesque stood up. He towered above the mayor and had to bend to say something — probably had to shout it — into the mayor's ear. Then he jumped down from the stage and started to move through the crowd. People pressed around him. I could see his lips move as he tried to answer questions that were being shouted at him, and to ignore some of the stupid accusations people were making.

I pushed my way through the mob to my mother, who was still near the front of the room.

"Well," she said to me, shaking her head, "that didn't go very well."

While we waited for the crowd around Levesque to thin, I looked for Phoebe. I didn't see her anywhere. Something told me that if I could locate Kyle, I'd find her, too. But Kyle wasn't in the room either.

After a few minutes, Mom sighed. "I think I'll wait outside," she said. "Interested in some ice cream?"

I shook my head. "I think I see Ross over there," I said. It wasn't true, but I didn't want to tell her that Caleb Darke had been lurking in our backyard. It would alarm her.

Mom nodded and headed for the door.

I looked at Levesque, who was in the middle of a smaller crush now. His smile was thin. The old woman was looking at him too. She was still frowning, but she didn't look thoughtful anymore. She was peering at him, and something in the way she was standing — leaning forward just a little — suggested that she was about to approach him. But she didn't. She didn't move from where she was standing.

I elbowed my way toward him and tugged on his arm. For what may have been the first time ever, he seemed happy to let me pull him away from work.

"Excuse me," he said to a woman who had been

shaking a finger at him. He rested a hand on my shoulder and steered me to a quiet — well, *deserted* — corner of the room, where I told him exactly what had happened. He examined me closely, as if searching for something bruised or broken. He seemed relieved to find me looking more or less as I had the last time he'd seen me.

"Was he armed?" he said.

"I don't think so." I hadn't seen a weapon, but he might have had one.

"And he was looking for me?"

I nodded.

"Do you have any idea where he went?"

I shook my head again. "Why would he show up at our house like that?" I said. What I meant was, if he hadn't attacked Jimmy Johnston, why had he been lurking at the back of the house? Why hadn't he come to the front door and rung the bell like anyone else? And if he had attacked Jimmy Johnston, why would he come to the house, where Levesque would have no choice but to arrest him and put him in jail, locked away from Terri?

Levesque silenced me with a sharp look. He glanced around at the angry faces of all the people who had come closer, still wanting to give him a piece of their mind. I shut my mouth immediately.

"Where's your mother?" he said.

"She went for ice cream."

"Find her," he said. "Tell her she'll have to make her own way home." Then, in a softer tone, "Apologize for me, okay?"

"Okay," I said.

I located Mom on the sidewalk, talking to her friend and my French teacher, Madame Benoit. When I delivered the message — without the background details — Madame Benoit offered to drive Mom home.

"I'll get home on my own," I told Mom. "I won't be late. I promise."

* * *

I ran into Ross half a block from the municipal building. He was tucking a reporter's notebook into the pocket of his cords.

"Covering this for school?" I said.

He shrugged. "Might be worth an editorial."

"*Might* be? A guy's rights are getting trampled, the Tysons are doing everything they can to drive him out of town, including inciting a lynch mob — and you think it *might* be worth an editorial?" I didn't mention that Caleb had shown up at my house.

"Hey, Caleb was convicted, you know."

"And he served his time. It's called *paying your debt to society*, Ross." He *had* paid his debt, I reminded myself. He had served his time.

I could have argued some more, but we would have ended up yelling at each other, and there had been enough yelling already. Ross must have felt the same way, because he didn't press me. In fact, he was looking at me sort of strangely, like he wanted to tell me something but was embarrassed or afraid to.

"What's up?" I asked.

"What do you mean?"

"Come on, Ross, I can read you like a newspaper."

"You want to go over to Stella's, maybe get something to eat?"

"Sure," I said. "Why not?"

He was quiet as we made our way along Centre Street. We found an empty booth and slid into it. Ross looked at the menu without really looking at it.

"Come on, Ross," I said. "Give it up."

Ross drew in a lungful of air, and then slowly blew it out again. He was just about to speak when Eric appeared.

"What are *you* doing here?" Ross said. His tone was less than friendly, which surprised me. I won't say that Ross and Eric are best buddies, but they have always seemed to be good colleagues. They both take the school newspaper seriously and they seem to work well together.

"I just came from the town meeting," he said. "I didn't see you there."

"I was standing near the back."

Eric slid into the booth beside me.

"Those people are too much," he said. "Especially the Tysons."

"They have every right to be angry," Ross said.

Eric scowled at him. "Come on," he said. "The Tysons decided they didn't like Caleb long before anything happened to Terri. Charles was the worst. He's such a hypocrite. He's always going on about all the trouble Caleb used to get into — as if he were any better."

"You mean the skinhead thing, right?" I said.

Eric nodded. "When Charles came back up here, he went out of his way to pick fights with Caleb. Or tried to. Caleb used to walk away. People forget that, though. Nobody ever mentions it."

Ross frowned. "What are you talking about?"

"Most of the fights between Charles and Caleb were started by Charles. And whenever he could, Caleb just walked away."

"Don't tell me," Ross said. "Let me guess: your uncle told you that, right?" Eric's uncle, the defence attorney.

"Right," Eric said, ignoring the sarcasm in Ross's voice. "But one time when Charles refused to let Caleb walk away, I was there."

We both stared at him.

"I was just a kid, but, boy, do I ever remember. I was walking home from school and I ran into them. Charles was goading Caleb, telling him to stay away from his sister or else. When Caleb tried to ignore him, Charles attacked him anyway. I've never seen anything like it. Makes you re-think those fights you see in the movies."

"What happened?" I asked.

"I ran to get the cops."

"And?"

Eric shook his head. "And they showed up and Charles said they were having what he called 'a friendly argument.' Caleb didn't contradict him, at least not while I was standing there. So, if you ask me, maybe there's more to Caleb than most people are willing to see. And even if you accept that Caleb did it, he served his time. What more do they want?"

Ross groaned. Eric looked sharply at him. Ross threw up his hands in surrender. "You don't have to argue with me," Ross said. "Chloe's already done that."

One of Stella's waitresses showed up. Ross ordered fries and gravy. Eric ordered a hamburger. I ordered coffee.

While we ate, Eric railed against the Tysons.

"Your step-dad's cool, though," he said. "Kyle told me what happened at Lawrence's. He said your step-dad helped to settle things with Mr. Lawrence."

At the mention of Kyle, Ross slumped lower in his seat. Eric looked across the table at him, fixing him with his blue-grey eyes.

"You and Kyle used to be close," he said.

"That was a long time ago," Ross said, staring down at his gravy-soaked fries.

Eric leaned forward. Something told me he was getting ready to lecture Ross.

"Whoa," I said, making a great show of checking the time. "I'd better get going before Mom sends out a search party." It wasn't *that* late, but I liked both Eric and Ross. I didn't want them to end up in a fight, which is where this was headed.

"I'll walk with you," Ross said, sliding out of the booth. He looked relieved to have an excuse to leave.

We walked the couple of blocks to Ross's house in

silence. Then I said, "Eric's right, isn't he?"

"Right about what?"

"You didn't just *know* Kyle. You two used to be friends. Good friends."

Ross glanced up at his house. "Wait here," he said. "I'll be right back." He walked up the driveway and let himself in the front door. I sat down on his porch steps and waited.

He was back in a few minutes with what looked like a shoebox.

"Gonna show me your new sneakers?" I said. He didn't answer. "Ross?"

He sighed, and it sounded like the regrets of a lifetime were filling the air around us. "He was here every day after school," he said.

He? "You mean Kyle?"

Ross nodded. "He loved it here. Mom wasn't working then. She'd do real mom stuff — you know, there'd be fresh muffins or warm cookies. On cold days, she'd make hot chocolate with marshmallows on top. He stayed for supper a lot, too."

He handed me the shoebox. I lifted the lid. There was a bunch of kid stuff in it — old action figures from movies I had all but forgotten, tiny metal cars and trucks, and a dozen or so photographs. I flipped through them, smiling. Ross and Kyle on skates, down at the lake. Ross and Kyle playing road hockey. Ross and Kyle in bathing suits, scarfing down hot dogs.

"Looks like you two were good friends."

"Yeah. *Were*. Best friends." He fingered one of the

photographs. "You were right," he said.

"You feel bad about it?"

He held out his hands and I gave him the shoebox. "Yeah," he said at last. "I do."

He stared down at the box before putting the lid back on. "I didn't think he even cared," he said. "All that stuff was happening about Caleb, and he just sort of kept to himself. His uncle used to pick him up after school every day. I thought that was the way he wanted it. I thought . . . " He looked down at the ground. I waited.

"Okay, so I told myself that was what he wanted. He never said anything about it to me, so I told myself that he didn't want to talk about it. To be honest, I was relieved. Nobody wanted to hang out with Kyle. And I wanted to be like everyone else." He sighed again. This time the sound was long and trembling. "I feel pretty ashamed of myself," he said.

"You were eight years old," I pointed out.

"*Then* I was eight years old."

I didn't say anything.

"Kyle's had it pretty rough," Ross said. "First his father died in a hunting accident. Then his mother died of cancer. Then his grandfather died."

Poor Kyle. Then, on top of everything, his brother was sent to prison.

"I heard it was Charles Tyson who shot Kyle's grandfather," I said.

"I don't know all the details," Ross said, "but I do know that there was an investigation. Caleb claimed it wasn't an accident, but that's the way it was ruled."

"Caleb thinks Charles did it on purpose?"

Ross nodded. Well, that went a little farther down the road to explaining the tension between the Darkes and the Tysons. It probably also explained Caleb's reaction in the back of the patrol car, when Charles had turned up at Jimmy Johnston's place. Mom was right. The Tysons and the Darkes were like the Montagues and the Capulets. Or maybe the Hatfields and the McCoys. It was a real family feud.

I glanced at Ross, who was staring down at the lid of the box.

"It's never too late, Ross," I said. I was trying to make him feel better. I'm not sure I believed it, though.

* * *

Mom was in the living room, with the TV on, when I opened the front door. From the look of anticipation on her face, quickly followed by one of disappointment, I decided that Levesque wasn't home yet. He was probably out looking for Caleb.

I kissed Mom good night and headed for my room. I hesitated when I got to the top of the stairs. I stared at Phoebe's closed door for a few seconds. Then I knocked.

"Can I come in?" I asked.

When I got no answer, I pushed open the door. Phoebe was sitting on her bed. Her eyes were pinkish and her mouth pouty. I'd have bet anything that she had been crying.

"The meeting was pretty bad, huh?" I said.

"I left before it ended," she said. "I couldn't stand it anymore. I used to like living here, but now I hate it. You should have heard what some people were saying."

"I know." I went right into the room and closed the door behind me. "Did you see Kyle tonight?"

She shook her head. "He wasn't there. And I'm glad he wasn't. I would have hated for him to hear all of that."

Maybe. But from what Ross had told me, I doubted any of it would have been news to Kyle.

"He likes you, doesn't he, Phoebe?" I said.

She stiffened. "*I* like *him*," she said. "So what?"

I told her what Levesque had said to Mom just before supper — that he didn't have enough information to figure out exactly who was lying and who was telling the truth about what had happened at Jimmy Johnston's camp. Had Caleb attacked Mr. Johnston and stolen some guns? Or had he really been with Kyle, as Kyle had claimed? "I bet Kyle knows where Caleb is," I said.

Phoebe looked down at her bed, not at me.

"If he knows," I said, "he should tell."

She stared at her bedspread as if it were a five-star movie.

That's when I decided to tell her. "Caleb was here tonight," I said.

That got her attention. "Here?"

"Out back. He told me to tell Levesque that he didn't do it. Then he said no one was going to keep him away from Terri. You know what that means, don't you?"

She shook her head.

"Geez, Phoebe," I said. "It means he's going to try to get to her again. Maybe he loves her and maybe he doesn't. But he's going to try to get to her and that's going to mean trouble. And he's in enough trouble already. If Kyle knows where Caleb is, he should tell. And if he doesn't want to tell, you should try to convince him."

She was shaking her head again.

"Phoebe, don't you get it?"

She looked at me blankly.

"Levesque isn't convinced that Jimmy Johnston is telling the truth. I don't know why, but he isn't. He said that he didn't have enough information to make up his mind one way or the other.

"First Daniel Tyson gets Caleb fired. Then Jimmy Johnston — Mr. Tyson's friend — says Caleb attacked him. They don't want him here. They're doing everything they can to get rid of him. I think Levesque knows that. The best way for Kyle to make sure they don't win is to convince Caleb to talk to Levesque. Then Levesque can figure out what really happened, who's really telling the truth. If Caleb really didn't do it, then he can trust Levesque. You should tell Kyle that. You should make sure he tells Caleb."

A great speech, I thought. One that got me precisely no answer. Kid sisters can be so irritating.

CHAPTER TWELVE

When I came out of school the next afternoon, more than ready for the weekend, I was surprised to find Ross and Phoebe standing together in the parking lot.

"What's up?" I said.

I didn't like the look that Phoebe gave Ross. It told me that the two of them knew something that I didn't. I focused on my sister.

"What's going on?" I said.

She glanced at Ross. Yup, they were definitely up to something.

"I asked Ross to drive me out to Kyle's place," Phoebe said at last. "You're right, Chloe. It would be best if Caleb talked to Dad. I was going to ask Kyle to tell Dad where Caleb is, but he wasn't at school today."

I was stunned. For once, my sister was actually taking my advice. And Ross, who as far as I knew hadn't had a conversation with Kyle in years, was going to take her out there.

"You want to come, right?" Ross said.

"Right," I said.

"We were waiting for you," Phoebe said.

Well, okay.

We piled into Ross's mom's Chev — Phoebe in the back, me up front next to Ross — and off we went.

"How come Kyle wasn't at school?" I asked her.

She shook her head. "Ever since Caleb got back to

town, Kyle hardly ever shows up. It's too bad, because exams aren't that far away and papers and projects are coming due. And up until recently, he had a good chance of passing."

I don't know why, but that surprised me. Like a lot of people, I'd always thought there was something odd about Kyle. He hardly ever looked up from his feet or his desk, and he hardly ever said a word, even when you asked him a direct question. I'd assumed that meant he wasn't too bright. And I'd assumed *that* meant he was doomed to fail, no matter what. I guess I was wrong. It seemed I'd been wrong about a lot of things, where the Darkes were concerned.

When we arrived at the Darke place, the old pickup I had seen the first time I was there was gone, but the green car was at the side of the house. Either someone was home or that car didn't work. The yard was empty and silent except for the engine of our car, and Ross killed that as soon as we pulled up in front of the sagging little house that Caleb and Kyle called home.

Phoebe jumped out and ran up onto the porch. I opened my door and got out, itching to run after her. But she was the one who had a special relationship with Kyle, not me. I was going to have to fight back my curiosity and let her do this on her own. Behind me I heard Ross's car door slam. In front, Phoebe was knocking — hammering — on the door.

"Kyle," she called. "Kyle, it's me."

The door creaked open. A head peeked out. Kyle's

head. Then he slipped through the crack in the door and stepped out onto the porch. A shy smile played across his face as he gazed at Phoebe. Phoebe beamed back at him for a moment before getting to the point of our visit.

"We want to talk to you," she said. "About Caleb."

Kyle peered over the top of Phoebe's head at Ross and me. He said something to Phoebe that I didn't hear. Then Phoebe turned to us and said, "I'll be back in a few minutes." She disappeared inside.

Phoebe was in the house for five minutes, ten minutes, more. Finally I couldn't stand it anymore. I started toward the steps. Just then, the door opened and Phoebe came out, followed by Kyle.

"We called Dad," she said. She turned to Kyle. "My dad's a good guy. If he can talk to Caleb, I know he can get everything straightened out."

Kyle didn't say anything. He didn't do anything, either. He just sat down on the porch step to wait. Phoebe sat down beside him. Ross perched on the hood of his mother's car. I leaned next to him.

I heard birds while we waited. I couldn't name any of them, although even I knew from the various calls and chirps that there were several different species out there, calling to each other. And then, finally, I heard something else. Car tires crunching over gravel. An East Hastings police car swung into view. It drew up alongside Ross's car and Levesque got out.

He surveyed the scene, processing Ross and me first, then Phoebe — sitting so close to Kyle that she seemed to be glued to his side. Phoebe nudged Kyle and the two of them stood up together. "I know where he is," Kyle said. "I can show you."

Levesque nodded to Kyle and the two of them moved away from us. They stood facing each other, Kyle almost as tall as Levesque, but slender as a sapling in contrast to Levesque's full-grown oak. Levesque was doing most of the talking, looking steadily into Kyle's eyes. And Kyle was looking straight back at him — not ducking his head to the ground the way he usually did, but nodding, shaking his head, answering questions. Then Levesque laid a hand on Kyle's shoulder and nodded.

"You kids stay here," he called to us. "Better yet — Ross, why don't you take the girls back to town?"

Kids? Girls?

Ross slid down off the hood of his mother's car. "If it's okay with you, we'd rather wait here," he said.

Even a bat could have seen that Levesque didn't think it was okay, but Ross pretended to have even worse vision than that. Levesque glowered at me — and I hadn't said a word. Then he said, "I mean it. You stay here."

I held up my hands in surrender. *Geez, lock me up and throw away the key, why don't you?*

Kyle and Levesque headed out of the clearing and were soon lost from sight in the surrounding bush.

I glanced at Phoebe, who looked sternly at me. "Don't even think about it," she said.

I thought about it, but I didn't act on what I was thinking.

Not until I heard the gunshot.

I jumped. Phoebe jumped. Ross jumped. Our heads snapped around in the direction of the *crack!* My first thought: *a car backfiring*. That's what we always used to say in the city. You'd hear a bang, you'd think, *Gunshot*, then you'd think, *Yeah, get real, it's a car backfiring*, unless it was three or four in the morning. Then maybe, *maybe*, it was a gunshot.

But we weren't in the city. We were in the middle of the bush, a couple of kilometres from the highway — from any road, in fact. The only two cars around were parked, their engines shut off. And, anyway, the sound had come from the bush.

Ross pushed away from the car and cocked his head to listen. I walked slowly to the edge of the clearing, where the yard ended and the bush began. So did the snaking trail that Kyle and Levesque had taken.

Phoebe called after me. "Where do you think you're going?"

Then I heard a voice, much fainter than Phoebe's, calling for help. That's when I started to run.

"Chloe!" Phoebe yelled.

I don't think she heard that other voice. Kyle's voice.

"Chloe, come back!" She had to yell, because by then I was running.

"Call someone," I shouted back over my shoulder. "Call Steve."

I didn't stop to think how stupid or dangerous it was to be heading in the direction of a gunshot. All

I thought was, *If Kyle is calling for help, then some-one has been hurt.*

Shot.

Three possibilities sprang to mind: Caleb, Kyle and Levesque. It was the last possibility that made my legs pump and my good sense shut down. Because if either Kyle or Caleb was the injured one, Levesque would already be in contact with Steve; he'd have the situation under control and there'd be no need for Kyle to be calling for help. At least that's what was racing through my brain as I dashed into the bush.

I ran down the path, my heart jackhammering in my chest. I ran, then I stopped and spun around. Which way? Which way?

"Help!" Kyle called again. "Over here! Help!"

"Kyle! Where are you? What happened?"

I heard someone thundering through the scrub behind me and turned to see Ross. I held a finger to my lips to stop him, so that I could hear Kyle's answer.

"Over here," Kyle said. His voice was coming from my left. "He's been shot. Your dad's been shot."

The warm, sunny day suddenly seemed chill and dark. I looked at Ross to see if he'd heard. He had. He sped toward me.

"We should go back," he said. "Phoebe phoned for help. We should wait back at the house."

"You go," I said. "I'm going to find Kyle."

"Bad idea," Ross said. He grabbed my arm to keep me from leaving. "Chloe, think! What if whoever did it is still out there? What if *you* get shot?"

I knew he was right. But still . . .

"Kyle, are you alone?"

"I'm with your dad," he called back.

I tried to pry Ross's fingers from my arm, but he held fast.

"You have to go back," I told him. "You have to make sure they send an ambulance."

He dug in his pocket and pulled out a cell phone. Mine was in my bag, in Ross's car. He punched in some numbers and started talking: 911, I realized. He was giving them additional information. Then he pressed *End* and tucked the phone back into his pocket.

"We should wait here," he said.

"You wait here if you want to. I want to see Levesque."

He didn't want to let go of me, but in the end he did.

"Kyle!" I called again. "Kyle, where are you?" When he answered, I blundered in the direction of his voice.

My feet were suddenly as heavy as blocks of cement, and as cold as the blood that was pushing its way sluggishly through my veins. Kyle was on his knees beside Levesque. Levesque was on his back, on the ground. It was a toss-up whose face was whiter. As I ran to them, I was desperately trying to remember what I had learned in first-aid class. What were those magic words the first-aid lady had worked so hard to hammer into our heads?

Emergency scene management. Four steps.

Step one: Scene survey. Find out what has happened.

"We were walking along the path," Kyle said. "I was taking him to Caleb and I heard a shot and I turned around and he went down, just like that."

Levesque's eyes were closed. Blood had blossomed, in a small patch, on the front of his shirt.

"Did you see who did it?"

Kyle shook his head. "I just heard the shot, and then I heard someone running. But I didn't see anything and I didn't want to leave your dad."

Okay. So whoever had shot Levesque had fled. Ross and Phoebe had called for help. Okay.

Step two: Primary survey. Assess the casualty for life-threatening injuries and give life-saving first aid.

He'd been shot. He was unconscious. Was he alive? The question leapt into my mind and I started to panic. Think.

Always think, the first-aid lady had said. *Always keep your wits about you.*

Assess the victim. Look for chest movement. Yes. Yes, there was some, but not much. *Listen for sounds of breathing and feel for breath on your cheek.* I bent over him. He was breathing. He was definitely breathing. Thank you. *Check for bleeding.* There was some of that. Lots of it, in fact. *Give life-saving first aid — in this case, try to stop or at least slow the bleeding.* My mind blanked. Think. *Think.*

I ripped off the denim shirt I was wearing over my T-shirt, folded it up inside out — working theory: the inside is cleaner than the outside — and pressed it over the wound on Levesque's chest. I applied as much pressure as I could. There were tears in my eyes when I looked back up at Kyle.

"You think it was Caleb, don't you?" he said, his voice a whisper.

In actual fact, I wasn't thinking anything. Mostly I was focusing on applying as much pressure as I could.

"You'd better go and meet Ross," I told him. "Someone should be coming soon."

Kyle stood up and started to back away from Levesque and me. For a moment, I wasn't sure what he was going to do, but then he turned and ran in the direction of his house. I looked down at my hands and my shirt. Blood was already soaking through, darkening the fabric. I pressed harder and ducked my head again to check that he was still breathing.

Part of my brain seemed to be working hard to convince me that this wasn't really happening. I felt the way you do when you wake up in a pitch-black room, screaming from a nightmare. You work at focusing, at telling yourself, *This isn't real*. But I felt my knees grinding into the hard-packed earth of the trail as I pushed down hard on my home-made compress. No matter how I tried to blink the picture away, I saw Levesque lying on the ground, eyes closed, face pale.

Face pale.

Shock?

The first-aid lady had gone on at great length about shock. I tried desperately to remember what she had said. *Symptoms: pale skin that turns bluish-grey.* I peered at Levesque. Pale, but not bluish. *Bluish-purple lips.* Nope. Not yet, anyway. *Cold and clammy skin.* I removed one hand from the compress — and almost went into shock myself when I saw all that blood. I looked in horror at my shirt. It was soaked almost all the way through. I wanted to scream for help, but what good would that do? *Always keep your head,* the first-aid lady had said. *You may be the only person who does.*

What was taking so long? Kyle's place was maybe a fifteen-minute drive from town. How long had it been since I'd told Phoebe to call? How long had it taken me to reach Levesque? How long had I been here? A total of ten minutes? Fifteen? More? How much blood had he lost? How much blood could a person lose and still keep breathing? How bad was the wound? Had the bullet hit anything important?

I took a deep breath, pressed a little harder and checked his breathing again. Was it my imagination, or did it seem shallower, more laboured? Then I whispered two words that, when I heard myself say them, scared me more than anything.

"Don't die."

Chapter Thirteen

Ross pulled me to my feet after Levesque had been lifted up onto a stretcher. I wiped my hands on the front of my jeans, smearing them with blood, then we ran back to Kyle's house. Steve Denby was there, ashen-faced.

"I called Jeanne Benoit," he said. "She's driving your mother up to Morrisville. I can arrange a ride for you two," he said to Phoebe and me.

"I'll take them," Ross said.

Steve looked relieved. I understood immediately. He wanted to get to work: find out who had shot Levesque — and why — and apprehend whoever it was.

Phoebe and I piled into Ross's car and we headed back toward the highway. I heard a snuffling sound behind me and turned my head. Phoebe was crying softly.

"Glove compartment," Ross said to me. "There should be some tissues."

I popped it open. Sure enough, there was a small box. I pulled a couple of tissues from it and passed them back to Phoebe.

"Don't cry," I said.

Not, *Don't worry*. Not, *It's going to be all right*. Not, *He's probably fine*. There were a lot of things I had fibbed about to my sister over the years, but there are a few things you don't lie about — ever. This was one of them.

The truth was, I was probably more worried than she was. After all, I had been there. I had seen all the blood. I had seen him go pale and then paler still. I had watched his breathing slow. By the time the ambulance attendants had arrived, I was pushing as hard as I could on the blood-soaked compress I had made out of my shirt. Tears were streaming down my cheeks. My hands were so covered in blood that Ross had wiped away my tears with the hem of his T-shirt.

We drove in silence all the way up to Morrisville. The same two words that I had whispered to Levesque kept running through my head: *Don't die. Don't die.*

Mom was at the hospital when we got there. She tried to look brave. She might have pulled it off, too, if it hadn't been for her watery eyes and the way she was sitting almost on the edge of her chair, her head snapping toward the waiting-room door every time someone came through it.

She hugged us both, which scared me — until she told us that she didn't know anything yet. Levesque was still in surgery.

And then we waited. Every now and then Mom squeezed my hand or Phoebe's hand or both of our hands together. Ross sat beside me. He got up a couple of times and went down the hall to fetch coffee and juice and soft drinks for whoever wanted them. I was working on a second cup of coffee when someone appeared in the door to the waiting room.

Five heads turned — Mom's and Jeanne Benoit's

and Phoebe's and Ross's and mine, because the truth was that Mom wasn't the only person who was worried sick. But it wasn't a doctor or nurse standing there. It was Kyle. Phoebe jumped up and ran over to him. He looked at all of us, but stayed where he was, even though Phoebe tried to pull him over to where we were sitting. In the end, I swung up out of my chair. Ross sighed and followed me. We went out into the hall with Kyle, who was looking back at Mom and Madame Benoit.

"That your mom?" he said to Phoebe.

Phoebe nodded.

Kyle looked at our mother again. Then he peered into Phoebe's eyes. "I'm sorry," he said. "I'm so sorry."

"It's not your fault," Phoebe said.

Kyle's eyes glistened. He seemed to be fighting back tears.

I glanced at Ross. I don't know what he was thinking, but the number-one question in my mind was, *What's going on with Kyle?* Sure, he was sorry Levesque had been shot. But, despite what Phoebe had just said to him, he was acting like maybe it was his fault. And was it my imagination, or had he not gotten around to saying that Caleb hadn't done it? I thought about what he had said back in the woods: *You think Caleb did it, don't you?* He hadn't protested his brother's innocence. He hadn't said, "He didn't do it." He had never said that — about anything, I now realized. He had only said that Caleb had served his time, paid his debt. Why was that?

Phoebe slipped her hand into Kyle's and they

walked down the hall together. I saw them standing in front of a display of teddy bears in the gift-shop window, talking intently. It hit me then that my kid sister was many things, but she wasn't a kid anymore.

My cell phone trilled. I scrambled in my bag and dug it out from under my wallet, my agenda, my brush, my keys . . . "Hello?"

"Chloe? It's Eric. I heard about your dad. How is he?"

I told him we were still waiting for news.

"Well, I've got some news for you," he said. "I'm downtown. I was going by the police station when I saw this old truck pull up and, Chloe, you'll never guess — "

"Caleb," I said. I'm not sure why I was so positive about it.

"Yeah," Eric said. "Caleb. He parked the truck and walked right into the police station. Apparently he said that he had heard your dad wanted to talk to him."

"You mean, he surrendered?" I said.

"All I know is what I told you."

"Was he arrested?"

"I tried to find out," Eric said. "I even asked Mr. Torelli." Mr. Torelli — editor of the *East Hastings Beacon*. "He didn't know either. But I heard they also found the gun that was used to . . . " His voice broke off. "It's a hunting rifle. But Steve isn't releasing any details yet."

A man in green surgical scrubs and a woman

from reception passed us on their way into the emergency waiting room. I saw the woman point. I saw my mother stand up as the man in surgical scrubs approached her.

"I gotta go, Eric," I said into the phone.

I saw hope and fear fight with each other in my mother's eyes, and I hurried to her side. She clutched my arm, and in that split second my whole world went black. *It's over,* I thought. *It's really over.*

Then my mother whispered, "Thank you," and I looked at her again and saw that relief had triumphed. "Can I see him?" she said.

"Soon," the doctor said. "We'll let you know when he's settled. He was extremely lucky, Mrs. Levesque. The bullet didn't hit anything vital."

Tears dribbled down my cheeks. When I glanced back toward the door, I saw alarm on Ross's face. I made myself smile through my tears. I hugged Mom, and then went to tell him the good news.

"He's going to be okay."

* * *

Mom went to see Levesque, but she wouldn't let us go with her. Not right away.

"Wait down here," she said, "until I see how everything is. Okay?"

I know Phoebe was as eager to see him as I was, but we both nodded. This was Mom's decision.

By the time Phoebe and I joined the guys, the news was all over the place. According to the East Hastings Police Department, Caleb Darke had been arrested for the stabbing assault on Jimmy Johnston — and was being investigated in the shooting of East Hastings Chief of Police Louis Levesque.

Kyle slumped against the wall when he heard the news. He looked defeated, but not at all surprised. "I can't believe Caleb would do this," he said. "He doesn't even like guns."

"We know Caleb didn't do it," Phoebe said, "don't we, Chloe?"

I considered Phoebe's question and pondered a few of my own.

Question number one: Why would Caleb calmly walk into the East Hastings police station shortly after he had supposedly shot Levesque and say that he had heard Levesque wanted to talk to him? Was that supposed to be some kind of alibi? *No, officer, I didn't shoot him. If I had shot him, would I be here now to talk to him?* I'm no genius, but even I could come up with something better than that.

Question number two: What motive did Caleb have to shoot Levesque? Sure, he had been accused of robbing and assaulting Jimmy Johnston. And, sure, that was serious. But Levesque had protected Caleb when he showed up in town. Yes, he had arrested him when he had trespassed at the Tysons', but he had also interceded on his behalf out at Jimmy Johnston's hunting camp. Caleb had to know that Levesque was fair. He had even come to the house looking for Levesque. Why would he all of a sudden decide to shoot him, when all

Levesque wanted was to talk to him?

And, finally, question number three: Why would Caleb have attacked Jimmy Johnston and stolen guns from him in the first place? Trespassing at the Tysons' was different. Caleb loved Terri, or at least he said he did. If he did love her, then he had been waiting eight years to see her. The Tysons, meanwhile, were doing everything they could to keep Caleb away, and Caleb knew it. Maybe he was frustrated. Maybe he had a bad temper. Maybe a lot of things. But I remembered the radiant look on Terri's face when Caleb had laid his hand on hers outside the daycare centre. And, well, it just didn't make sense that a guy who had declared that no one was going to make him go away *ever again* would stab one man and shoot another. Assault and attempted murder were a sure-fire recipe for being sent away — for a very long time. It didn't add up.

"Chloe?" Phoebe said. "Did you hear what I said? *We* know Caleb is innocent, don't we?"

"Yeah," I said to Kyle. "The thing is, though — " Beside me, Ross drew in a sharp breath. I knew he was afraid of what I might say. *Thanks a heap.* "If Caleb didn't do it, then who did?" I said.

"And why?" Ross added wearily.

* * *

Phoebe and I were allowed to see Levesque for a few minutes. It seemed like a few seconds, and a whole lifetime, all at the same time. We stood beside his bed. He was hooked up to all kinds of monitors. There were tubes everywhere. His face was pale. His eyes were closed. His chest barely seemed to move as he breathed.

I kept flashing back to the woods, when I was pressing as hard as I could on his chest — terrified that it wasn't enough, that I wasn't going to be able to make the difference.

Beside me, Phoebe was sniffling and leaking tears. Then Mom hustled us out of the room and told us that she was staying, but that she wanted us to go home. Did we think we could manage without her for the rest of the evening, and maybe for tomorrow too? We told her we could. We promised that if we needed anything, we would call Madame Benoit. We told her that we would get Ross or Madame Benoit to drive us back to the hospital tomorrow and that if we couldn't catch a lift, we would take the bus. We made her promise to call us if anything happened.

Kyle had driven up to the hospital in the ancient green car I had seen parked beside his house. Phoebe offered to ride back with him. At first Kyle didn't want her to, but she insisted. Phoebe insisting is like wind working on limestone — she eventually wears you down. Kyle relented and said he'd make sure she got home safely. I drove home with Ross. When we got to my house we sat in the driveway, the car engine idling, and looked at each other.

"Right," Ross said, putting the car into reverse.

As he backed up the car, I said, "Where are we going?"

"To the police station," he said. "That's what you want, isn't it?"

I felt like hugging him. "Ross, I think you're the best friend I've ever had."

He beamed all the way into town.

* * *

Steve Denby was on the phone when we pushed open the door of the East Hastings police station. He gave me a Levesque-like look. In other words, he didn't exactly seem thrilled to see me in his place of business. Ross and I stayed back by the door until he had finished his phone call.

"What can I do for you, Chloe?" he said, replacing the receiver in its cradle. I swear he had been taking lessons from Levesque. Drop his voice an octave and he could have *been* Levesque.

"You talked to Mom, right?" I said. "You know he's going to be okay, right?"

He nodded and couldn't hide his relief, no matter how stern he tried to look.

"Do you think Caleb did it?" I said.

"Chloe, you know what the chief would say — "

"It's just one question, Steve," I said.

But he was shaking his head before I even got to the end of my sentence. "I'm going by the book on this one, Chloe," he said. "I'm going to do just what the chief would do if he were here, and I'm not going to do anything that he wouldn't do. I'm sorry."

Not nearly as sorry as I was.

"I heard you arrested Caleb," I said, pushing a little more — or trying to.

Steve crossed his arms over his chest. Ross nudged me. Ross was a lot less stubborn than me. But this time he was right. Steve had made up his mind. He had decided that he wasn't going to tell me anything, and this wasn't the best time to try to change his mind. I walked out of the police station, trailed closely by Ross. We headed over to Stella's and claimed a booth near the back. Ross ordered a Coke and a hamburger. I ordered coffee.

"So," he said, slurping his drink through a straw while I stirred a splash of milk into Stella's no-nonsense, no-cappuccino coffee. "You going to start running it down?"

"What are you talking about?"

"Right. Like I can't hear the gears grinding and the wheels turning up there." He pointed at my forehead. "I know you, Chloe. We've done this before. It's going around and around in your mind — if Caleb didn't do it, then someone else must have. Stands to reason, right?"

Well, yeah, it did.

"Who else would have shot your step-dad? And why? Right?"

"Right."

"So, go," he said, holding up an index finger.

I stared down into my coffee for a moment. "Okay, there's Charles and Daniel Tyson," I said.

Ross popped his middle finger up beside his index finger. Suspects one and two.

"Motive?"

"They both hate Caleb. They both want him out

of town. They both knew Levesque was looking for Caleb to question him about the stabbing of Jimmy Johnston," I said. "It's possible one of them shot at Levesque to frame Caleb. You know, to make it look like Caleb shot Levesque so that he would be arrested again and sent back to prison."

"Except that they would have had to know that Levesque was out in the woods near the Darkes' place at that exact time," Ross said. "And how could anybody know that? Your dad didn't know himself that he'd be there, until Phoebe called him. And I don't think Phoebe knew for sure that *she'd* be there until I said I'd drive her."

"Maybe after Phoebe called him, he told someone where he was going. Probably he told Steve. Maybe someone else found out and followed him."

Ross looked far from convinced. "Someone would have had to follow him, show up at the Darkes' place without being seen, track him and Kyle into the woods and then shoot at him. And get away without being seen. How likely is that?"

"I don't know," I said honestly. "You're the one who's lived up here all his life. How likely is it?"

One of Stella's waitresses slid a plate in front of Ross. A hamburger, garnished with a slice of onion and a slice of tomato, nestled between a mound of French fries and a little paper cup filled with coleslaw. Ross salted his fries and dashed them with vinegar. Then he set to work on the ketchup bottle, whapping it and thwacking it, trying to get it to give up some ketchup.

"It's possible, I guess," he said. *Whap-thwack.* "*If* someone knew the area around the Darkes' place well enough. And *if* they knew where Levesque was going, so that they could get there without him seeing them. And *if* they had a rifle and *if* they were a fairly accurate shot — assuming they actually meant to hit him and not just scare him." *Whap-thwack.*

"Scare Levesque?" I said, snorting. The man was fearless. Then I sobered, realizing that if whoever had shot Levesque hadn't meant to scare him, then he had meant to hit him. Any way you looked at it, when you aimed to shoot someone, you were aiming to do some serious damage. I wondered what kind of shots Charles and Daniel Tyson were.

"There's Jimmy Johnston," I said. "He doesn't like Caleb any better than the Tysons do. Caleb has already been in at least one fight with him. *And* he claims Caleb stabbed him and stole guns from him. I bet he wasn't happy that Levesque hadn't arrested Caleb on that charge yet. And he runs a hunting camp, so he can probably track and shoot, right?"

Whap-thwack. Ross nodded at what I had said. *Whap-thwack.* The ketchup bottle released its grip on its contents and ketchup flooded over Ross's fries. I had to turn away for a minute. It looked too much like blood.

"Then there's that guy who *works* for Jimmy Johnston who doesn't like Caleb very much, either," I said. I told Ross what had happened when Levesque and I had gone to Johnston's hunting camp.

"You think Steve is checking them out?" Ross

said between mouthfuls of burger and fries.

I shrugged. I was sure Steve was doing whatever he could to find out who had shot Levesque. But what if he thought he already knew? What if he thought he had the culprit in custody? There have been plenty of cases of police making an arrest and thinking they have it all nailed down and, because of that, they stop investigating. *You have to keep an open mind,* Levesque always says. *You can't reach a conclusion too quickly, not until all the questions have been answered.* "All the questions" included method, opportunity and motive.

Method? If Caleb had stolen those rifles from Jimmy Johnston's place, then he sure had a method.

Opportunity? Hadn't Levesque been on his way to talk to Caleb? Someone — Steve, for example — could argue that Caleb had seen him coming and panicked.

And motive? Maybe Caleb thought he was going to be arrested again. Maybe he thought he was in danger of being charged with robbery, and assault with a dangerous weapon. Maybe he thought that, with his record, his next stop would be prison — again. If that was what Steve thought, he'd stop looking for another suspect. If Caleb hadn't done it, that would be bad for him, but very good for whoever had shot Levesque.

"Now what?" Ross said.

I glanced at my watch. It was getting late. "Now I guess I go home."

"I'll drive you," Ross said.

I smiled at him. "Then I get some sleep. Then, tomorrow, I go back up to Morrisville to see Mom and Levesque."

He waited. When I didn't continue, he said, "And?" as if my list was incomplete. Which, of course, it was.

"And I figure out how to get Steve to look into other possibilities besides Caleb, if he isn't already doing that," I said.

* * *

After Ross dropped me off, I found Phoebe sitting in the kitchen, her cheeks damp with tears.

"Hey," I said, slipping into a chair next to her, "he's going to be fine. You heard what the doctor said."

"I know," Phoebe said. She wiped her tears with the back of her hand. I reached for a box of tissues and passed it to her. "But who would want to shoot him? And don't you dare say it was Caleb."

"I don't think it was him at all," I said. I laid out my thinking for her. It seemed to make her feel better. "Ross said he'd drive us to Morrisville tomorrow morning," I told her.

"Do you think he'd pick up Kyle on the way?"

"Why?" I said. "You don't want to drive up there alone with him?"

Her face turned pink. "There's something wrong with his car," she said. "It stalled twice on the way back."

"Uh-huh," I said.

She turned pinker.

We both went upstairs: her to her room, me to mine. I don't know what was on Phoebe's mind that night, but I thought about Levesque.

When I had first met him, I hadn't liked him — mostly because he was always on my case. And then, of course, he had dragged us all up here to East Armpit, which hadn't improved my overall impression of him. But now I had a jumble of pictures in my mind. Levesque, standing between squabbling parties, listening, watching, talking quietly, making peace. Levesque standing at the stove, an apron tied around his waist, stirring a pot of spaghetti sauce while Mom gazed adoringly at him. Levesque in the audience at Phoebe's last debate, nodding his approval and then presenting her with half a dozen roses when it was over — because, he'd said, he had known she was going to win. Levesque coming to my rescue — not once, but a couple of times. The look of genuine relief on his face when he'd checked me out to make sure I was okay.

That's when I started to cry. I don't remember when I fell asleep.

CHAPTER FOURTEEN

Steve Denby shook his head when he spotted me heading toward him. He was in the second-floor hospital waiting room with my mother. Unlike Steve, Mom looked happy to see me — and Phoebe and Ross, and even Kyle.

"How's Dad?" Phoebe asked.

"Tired," Mom said. "He needs a lot of rest. But he's going to be fine."

"Can I see him?"

"Sure, you can." Mom glanced at Ross and Kyle.

"We'll wait here," Ross said. "Right, Kyle?"

Kyle nodded.

Mom and Phoebe started down the hall toward Levesque's room. When I didn't follow, Mom looked back at me.

"I'll be right there," I told her.

She nodded. After she had vanished, I turned to Steve again —

"No, Chloe," he said.

"You don't even know what I'm going to say."

Steve glanced at Ross and Kyle.

"Yes, I do," he said, his voice just above a whisper. "And I don't need you or anyone else to tell me how to do my job."

"It wasn't Caleb," I said.

Steve glanced at Kyle before shooting me an angry look, as if to say, *Now look what you've got me into.* "I have to get back to work," he said, and headed for the elevator.

I looked at Ross. I had been up half the night worrying about Levesque and wondering about Caleb. The more I thought about it, the more it didn't make sense that Caleb had shot Levesque. He had nothing to gain by it, and everything to lose. Which meant that someone else must have done it. But why? Just to get Caleb out of town and away from Terri? Or was there another reason? Suppose Caleb *had* been innocent all along. Then suppose someone *else* had attacked Terri. Now that Caleb was back in town, was that person nervous?

"I'm going to go see Levesque," I said. "Then we can talk about how we're going to help Caleb."

"Help Caleb?" Kyle said.

"Yeah," Ross said. He peered hard at Kyle, like he was looking at someone from the distant past — someone whose acquaintance he wanted to renew. "I'm with Chloe," he said. "I don't think Caleb shot the chief." I noticed that he didn't say he believed Caleb hadn't stabbed Jimmy Johnston or beaten Terri Tyson to within an inch of her life. But then, Kyle hadn't said those things, either.

I left them together in the waiting room and went down the hall to find Levesque. He had a room to himself. Mom and Phoebe were sitting in chairs on either side of the bed. Mom was holding his hand. He was hooked up to an IV. He looked paler than I have ever seen him, he could have used a shave and he sure looked tired. But he managed a limp smile when he saw me and — who knew this would happen? — I could hardly breathe for the lump in my throat, and I could hardly see because my eyes were filling with tears. I had to work hard to keep them in check.

"Hi," I said.

"Hi," he said. He seemed to have to make an effort just to get that one word out, but he didn't stop there. "The ambulance guys, they said you did a good job. Thanks."

That did it. I was officially crying. Mom handed me some tissues and I blotted at my eyes. Phoebe and I stayed a few minutes longer, then Mom hustled us back out into the hall. "He's really tired," she said. "He needs to rest."

"What about you, Mom?" I said. She had dark circles under her eyes. I wondered how much sleep she had got the night before.

"I'm staying here," she said. "At least for a while. You two are okay, right?"

"Of course we are," I said. I thought about telling her that she needed as much rest as he did, that she should look after herself. Then I thought about the way she looked at Levesque, and how much she smiled now that he was part of her life, and I bit my tongue. If she wanted to worry, that was fine with me. In her place, I'd probably do the same. And if she wanted to stick to him like a burr, that was okay, too. "Phoebe has her cell phone," I said. "And I have mine. You can call us any time. We'll be back tomorrow. And don't worry. We'll be fine."

Mom hugged us. She was sitting on a chair beside the bed when we left, holding Levesque's hand again and watching him while he slept.

We met Kyle and Ross back in the waiting area. Phoebe caught hold of one of Kyle's arms and they strolled toward the entrance together. I walked with Ross.

"How is he?" Ross said as we passed the nurses' station.

But I didn't answer because something had caught my ear. Someone had said Levesque's name. When I turned to look, I saw it was an elderly woman. The woman I had seen in the parking lot at Benny's, and again at the meeting where Levesque had answered questions about Caleb.

"I'm sorry," a nurse was telling her, "but I'm not allowed to give out any information."

The woman looked so disappointed that I left Ross and went over to talk to her.

"My name is Chloe," I told her. "Louis Levesque is my step-father. Is there something I can do for you?"

"I'm Amelia Brown," she said. "How is he?"

"He's going to be okay," I told her. "I think he's going to be in here for a while, though. Do you want me to tell him that you were here?"

She shook her head. "I don't actually know him," she said, "other than having seen him around town, of course. But I was here visiting a neighbour and I heard about what happened and, well . . . " She shrugged. "I hope your step-father gets well soon, dear," she said. As she made her way down the hall, I turned to Ross.

"Do you know her?" I asked.

"Mrs. Brown? Sure. I've seen her around. She lives outside of town. She and her husband used to run a stable. You know, horseback riding. Mostly during the tourist season."

"Used to?"

"He died a couple of years ago. I think she mostly boards horses now."

* * *

"Maybe Steve is still investigating," Ross said out in the parking lot, where we had met up with Phoebe and Kyle. Good old Ross, always on the side of law and order. Especially order — as in *a place for everything, everything in its place, and let's follow standard operating procedure here, shall we, folks?* We were trying to decide what to do next.

I rolled my eyes at what Ross had said. "Last I heard, Caleb was still in custody," I said. Kyle confirmed this.

"Okay," Ross said. "Okay, so maybe he isn't investigating." He stared down at his feet for a moment, then back up at me. "What do we do now?"

"We start by finding out where Charles and Daniel Tyson and Jimmy Johnston were yesterday afternoon when Levesque was shot."

A look of disdain washed over Kyle's face at the mention of those names. Who could blame him? "It was a big mistake for Caleb to think he could marry Terri," he said.

"I thought you liked Terri," Phoebe said.

So had I — although to be honest, I wasn't sure why I had thought that. I realized I had just assumed it because everyone else seemed to like her so much.

"I did," Kyle said. But he wasn't looking at either Phoebe or me. Instead, he was looking down at the ground.

"But . . . ?" I said it gently, but that didn't stop Phoebe from slipping one of her hands into one of Kyle's, as if she needed to give him support. Against me. "But what, Kyle?" I said.

"But nothing," he said. "Except that if it hadn't been for her, none of this would have happened. Caleb wouldn't have gone to prison. Everyone wouldn't be against him now. Your father wouldn't be in the hospital."

Phoebe stepped closer to him.

"Caleb was . . . is . . . in love with her," I said.

"He would never have asked her out," Kyle said. "It was all her idea. He was her project."

"Project?"

"Never mind," Kyle said. He turned away from me. I glanced at Phoebe. She was frowning. Wondering.

"What do you mean, *project*?" she said. She tugged on Kyle's hand.

When Kyle turned to look at her, it was like she was his universe. His eyes met hers and the anger on his face vanished. He raised one of his hands and touched her cheek. She smiled at him. Kyle put an arm around her before answering her question.

"Caleb dropped out of school. He hated it. Said it made him feel stupid. Grandfather said it was more stupid to quit. He pushed Caleb to finish, to take correspondence courses. He went to the school to see if he could get a tutor for Caleb, to help him get through."

"And the tutor was Terri?" I said.

Kyle nodded. "She used to come out to the house every day to bug him."

"Bug him?"

"He didn't want a tutor. He didn't want to finish school. But the more he said no, the harder she tried to get him to say yes. Grandfather said some people are like that — they think that if they just try hard enough, they can save people who don't want to be saved. Terri pestered him and pestered him and the next thing you know . . . " He shrugged. "She should have left him alone."

I didn't know what to say. Neither did Phoebe. It was Ross who finally broke the silence. "So," he said, "how are we going to do it?" When we all turned to look at him, he elaborated. "How are we going to find out where everyone was yesterday afternoon?"

I had to admit, it wasn't going to be easy. There were some other things that wouldn't be easy either. Things that I wished I could let ride, except that I couldn't. I had to know.

"Kyle? When Terri was . . . attacked . . . where was Caleb?"

Kyle stiffened, ready to defend himself and his brother. "He said he was over at the Browns', cutting wood."

"The Browns'?" I said. "You mean, the stables?"

Kyle nodded. "He worked for Mr. Brown sometimes, doing odd jobs. He said he was there when Terri was attacked."

"So he had an alibi," Phoebe said. She looked confused. "That must have come out at the trial."

"It did," Kyle said. "Caleb said he was at Mr. Browns' place until six-thirty. Uncle Thaddeus had dropped him off that morning with his bicycle, because Caleb's old car was having engine trouble." I wondered if it was the same old car Kyle now drove. "Caleb was going to ride his bike home. It would have taken him at least a half an hour to get to town from the Brown place. That meant that he couldn't have been at the Tysons' at twenty minutes to seven, which is when Mrs. Tyson said she came home and heard a scream and scared off whoever was attacking Terri."

"Did Mrs. Tyson see who it was?"

Kyle shook his head. "Whoever it was, she scared them off."

"But the alibi?" Phoebe said. "What happened to Mr. Brown and the alibi?"

"Mr. Brown testified that Caleb left at six o'clock, which *would* have given him enough time to get to the Tysons'. He said Caleb told him that he was going to meet Terri after work. He also said that Caleb told him Terri had something to tell him, and that it was important."

"Did he say what it was?" Everyone had said Caleb attacked her because she was going to break up with him.

Kyle looked down at the ground. It shouldn't have surprised me. I knew Kyle as a guy who hardly ever looked up. But this time, as I watched him and listened to him, I got the feeling that he was avoiding my eyes because he was hiding something.

"Caleb says he never found out," he said. "He says he never met her that night."

There it was, the thing that was bothering me. *Caleb says.* Kyle had said it over and over again. *Caleb said this* and *Caleb said that.* I thought about what I would say if someone were questioning me about a brother who had been sent to prison for something he hadn't done. I would say, *He didn't do it.* Kyle was saying that *Caleb said* he didn't do it.

"The jury believed Mr. Brown," Kyle said. "Not Caleb."

Phoebe squeezed Kyle's hand again.

I thought about Mrs. Brown — about how she had shown up at Benny's parking lot but kept her distance from the angry crowd. She had been at the town forum too, and again distinguished herself from everyone else by her calm. I wondered what she had been thinking, both times.

"Kyle, does Caleb know how to use a rifle?" I said.

Phoebe gave me a stern look. Her mouth started

to open. She was getting ready to blast me. I ignored her.

"Does he, Kyle?"

Kyle nodded.

"Even though he doesn't like guns?" I said.

"Chloe — " Phoebe began.

"That *is* what you said yesterday, right, Kyle?" I said. "That Caleb doesn't like guns?"

Phoebe's expression hardened into fury. I heard Ross shuffling uneasily beside me.

"Yeah," Kyle said. "So what?" His black eyes zeroed in on mine. I was starting to understand that there was one thing that could turn shy, quiet, odd Kyle into a tiger — and that was the subject of his brother. "After what happened to my father, Caleb had problems," he said. "So what? Who wouldn't?"

"What kind of problems?" I had to force myself not to look at Phoebe. Something told me that if I did, I'd turn to stone.

"Nightmares," Kyle said. "Trouble at school. The usual stuff. He also couldn't stand to be around guns, which was a problem."

I waited. Maybe I was wrong, but I sensed that Ross and Phoebe were waiting too. Like me, they wanted to know more.

"Our grandfather did a lot of guiding work back when we were kids, before Jimmy Johnston's place really took off. He had a lot of guns around. After what happened to Dad, Caleb tried to trash them all. Grandfather got really angry. He hauled Caleb out back and wouldn't let him leave until he learned to shoot. Then he taught him — taught us both — about gun safety."

"'Guns don't kill people, *people* kill people,'" Ross muttered.

Phoebe turned her fiery eyes on him.

"So, yeah," Kyle said. "Caleb knows how to use a rifle. And he's pretty good with targets. Grandfather saw to that. But he never hunted. He wouldn't even go into the woods during hunting season unless he was visible for at least a mile."

I didn't know whether I believed that or not, but at least I knew a little more about Caleb. And it had answered one of my questions. I had just one more. It was even harder to ask. "Where was Caleb when Jimmy Johnston was stabbed?"

"Chloe!" Phoebe said. "Kyle already told you that Caleb was with him."

I didn't look at my sister. I kept my eyes steady on Kyle. "Was he?" I said. "Tell the truth, Kyle."

Nothing.

"I believe Caleb loves Terri," I said. "I *don't* believe he shot Levesque." I let him think about that. "Where was he when Jimmy Johnston was stabbed and those guns were stolen?"

Kyle bowed his head for a moment, but when he answered, he looked directly at me.

"He says he was in the bush," he said.

"Where in the bush?"

Kyle rocked from foot to foot. "A place," he said.

"What place?"

Kyle looked over at Phoebe. I think he was trying

to decide how much things were worth to him. Phoebe, Caleb, peace, truth.

"My grandfather's cabin," he said at last. "It's way back in the bush. Caleb knows where it is. So do I. I think everyone else has pretty much forgotten it exists." He scuffed at the pavement with the toe of his sneaker. "He and Terri talked about living there. Caleb sure liked it back there. Terri was working on fixing the place up, before . . . " He paused and shook his head, clearing it of old memories, I think. "Caleb went back there after Mr. Lawrence fired him."

"Did he ask you to lie about where he was?"

Kyle shook his head. "When Mr. Johnston said Caleb had attacked him, Caleb didn't think anyone would believe him. I just wanted — "

"To help him?" I said.

He nodded.

"If you want to help him, you have to tell the truth," I said. "And you have to let *Caleb* tell the truth."

Phoebe pressed closer to Kyle. "My dad will believe him," she said. "My dad's fair."

All of which was true. Levesque was all that. But he wasn't in charge at the moment.

"You have to tell Steve," I said.

It took another few moments, but Kyle finally nodded.

* * *

I knew for a fact that Charles Tyson never worked on Saturdays. I knew because my mother told me every time she pulled a Saturday shift. *A boss should never make an employee do something he isn't prepared to do himself,* she would say. Mom didn't like working Saturdays. She liked working Sundays even less.

So I knew, when the glass doors parted for me that afternoon, that there was no chance that I would run into Charles. I headed for his office anyway, because I knew that Shirlene Sylva would be there. Shirlene was the assistant manager. When Charles wasn't in the store, she was. That meant she worked every Saturday and Sunday. When she wasn't strutting around the store making sure everything was shipshape, she could be found sitting in Charles's leather swivel chair, drawing up schedules and checking sales reports.

"Hi, Shirlene," I said, poking my head through the door. All the staff at the East Hastings Canadian Tire wear little tags sporting their first names, and everyone expects you to call them by those names — everyone except Mr. Tyson.

"Chloe," she said. The leather moaned gently as she sank back in the swivel chair. "How's your stepdad?"

"He's going to be okay," I said. "Mom's staying with him pretty much twenty-four hours a day, though."

Shirlene gave me a sympathetic smile.

"Anyway," I said, "she sent me over because she was supposed to drop this by for Charles yesterday afternoon." Mom had Fridays off. "But she never made it, you know, what with all the excitement." I held out an envelope on which I had carefully printed Charles's name. Underneath, in big block letters, it said, *PERSONAL AND CONFIDENTIAL.*

She took the envelope from me, read the words on the front, then turned it over. It was obvious that she was dying to know what was inside.

"He wasn't mad that she forgot, was he, Shirlene?"

"Huh?" She tore her eyes from the envelope and looked back up at me. "Gosh, no, I don't think so," she said. "He wasn't even here yesterday afternoon."

"Oh? Because Mom gave me the impression he wanted that by the end of the day or else." I nodded at the envelope.

She shook her head. "That's news to me," she said. "All I know is that for once in his life he took off around lunchtime, and he didn't come back until, oh, just before closing, I think." Canadian Tire closed at nine. She turned the envelope over and over in her hands. "I'll see that he gets this, though."

I nodded, then bit my lower lip to make it look like I was really struggling.

"Maybe I'd better let Mom give it to him after all," I said. I took the envelope back. "Maybe it would be better if she explained to him why she didn't give it to him when she was supposed to."

I could see Shirlene was dying to know what *it* was. But she didn't ask. At least, she didn't ask *me*.

I had no doubt that she would ask Charles, and then they would both be perplexed.

I headed down to Stella's to wait for Phoebe and Ross.

Phoebe arrived first. She was flushed. She slid breathlessly into the seat opposite me and bounced up and down so much that I wasn't sure that the coffee she'd ordered was a good idea.

"So?" I asked her.

"So, I checked it out," she said. "First I had to make sure that Mr. Tyson wasn't at the bank. Then I asked for his assistant."

"And?"

"And they should give me an Academy Award," Phoebe said, beaming. "I told her that I had arranged to interview Mr. Tyson yesterday afternoon for my Careers project, and that I was *mortified* because I had missed my appointment. I actually used that word — mortified. His assistant looks like she's close to retirement. I think she liked that 'mortified' was in my vocabulary."

"Great, Pheebs." You know what they say — it's the details that lend verisimilitude. Well, okay, so maybe *they* don't say that. Maybe it was my grade-nine English teacher back in Montreal who had said that, and a ton of other polysyllabic words besides. What it comes down to is this: if you're going to lie, make it a good story with plenty of details. "And?"

"And she said, 'Well, we can't have that, can we?' Then guess what she said?"

I decided to take a stab at it. "She said that she wouldn't worry about apologizing, because Daniel Tyson wasn't even at the bank yesterday afternoon."

My stab deflated Phoebe. "How did you know?" she said.

I shrugged. "Lucky guess. Did she know where he'd been?"

Phoebe perked up again. "That's the thing. She didn't. She seemed quite put out about it too. She said he'd had a number of other appointments scheduled and that she'd had to apologize for all of them. She said he's usually in on Saturdays too, but he'd called to say he wouldn't be in today — and he didn't explain why he missed his appointments yesterday."

I stared at my sister. "She told you all that?"

Phoebe grinned at me. "Well, when she said he wasn't there yesterday afternoon, she seemed kind of annoyed. So I said, 'It must be hard, being someone's assistant and having to keep track of them and everything.'" The sympathy ploy. I'd used it myself. "That's when she told me. I have the feeling she doesn't get enough appreciation."

I was filling Phoebe in on what I had found out at Canadian Tire when Ross appeared, looking pale and shaken.

"Never again," he said as he flopped down into the booth beside me. "I mean that, Chloe. Phoebe, you're a witness. Never again will I go asking questions for you in a place where they not only *have* guns, they walk around *carrying* guns."

Ross was the only one of us who had a driver's license, so we had dispatched him to Jimmy Johnston's hunting camp.

"And?" I said.

"'Gee, sorry to hear you had a rough time, Ross,'" Ross said, in a not-very-flattering imitation of me. "There's this guy who works for Johnston. Tough-looking guy named Pip. What kind of stupid name is that, anyway?"

"Actually, it's the name of the main character in *Great Expectations*," I said. "You know, the book by Charles Dickens."

"Yeah. Well, I bet *that* Pip wasn't a Rottweiler on two legs. This one was. He was in my face before I was even out of the car. He gave me the third degree. Wouldn't even let me see Mr. Johnston."

"And?" I said. I was fighting to keep from grinning. I felt for Ross, I really did. I had seen Pip. And Ross was right, there was a lot of Rottweiler in the guy. Pip had been itching to pop Caleb, and Caleb stood almost a whole head taller than him. But a picture of Ross, quaking and shaking, flashed in my mind — and for some perverse reason, it made me want to laugh.

Ross drew in a deep breath. "I gave him my spiel: I'm working on a story for the *Beacon* and I had arranged to speak with Mr. Johnston yesterday afternoon, but I got held up at school, et cetera, et cetera. He looked at me like I was from Jupiter — "

"Mars," I said. "People look at you like you're from Mars."

"Whatever," Ross said. He sounded truly annoyed. "Did I mention the guy was carrying a gun? He was cleaning it when I drove up and when he came over to the car, he had it slung under his arm, you know, like some hillbilly cop in one of those cheesy action movies. So there he was, his rifle half pointed at me, half pointed at the ground, and he says, 'What're you trying to pull, kid? You never had no arrangement to speak with Jimbo.' He told me, 'Jimbo don't speak to reporters.' I think that was my big mistake, saying I was with the *Beacon*."

Ross's hands were shaking when he reached for the glass of water that I hadn't touched. He gulped some down. "He said if I'd had a meeting with Jimmy Johnston, he would have known about it. I told him he must be mistaken."

I could see that going over really well with the Pipster.

Ross gulped some more water. "The guy got right in my face, Chloe. Right in my face! He demanded to know what time the appointment was for. I said four-thirty." Which was approximately when Levesque had been shot.

"And?"

"He said Jimbo had left by then."

"He said that? He'd left?" Interesting. "Did you ask where he went?"

"You're kidding, right?" Ross said. "You expected me to ask him that?" The rest of the water vanished down Ross's throat. "I tried to arrange to speak with Mr. Johnston again, you know, to make it look good — to make it look like I wasn't lying, and didn't deserve to be shot on the spot. Then I got out of there. Fast." He slumped against the back of the booth, exhausted.

"Well," I said, "we know more than we did a few hours ago." Specifically, we knew that Charles and Daniel Tyson hadn't been where they were supposed to have been on Friday afternoon, and no one seemed sure why. And we knew Jimmy Johnston had left the lodge some time before four-thirty, which was just before Levesque had been shot.

"Yeah," Ross said. "We know where some people weren't. But we don't know where they all were. How does this help us, Chloe?"

It was a good question. One that I decided to dodge for the moment.

CHAPTER FIFTEEN

Phoebe went home to catch up on some homework, which was just like her. She recorded all of her homework assignments in the agenda she had bought before school even started. She ticked off each assignment when she completed it. She had a system, which she had picked up at school: research, outline, draft, rewrite, polish, proofread, final version. Phoebe was a rule-book type of person, whether the rules applied to sports, grammar or personal organization. She would make a first-class accountant or train scheduler or air-traffic controller. More power to her.

I also had assignment deadlines looming, but I didn't head home to work. Instead, I trudged down to the East Hastings Public Library. I didn't go there to slog through assignments, though. I went to look at microfilm containing back issues of the *East Hastings Beacon*. Ross and Eric had told me bits and pieces of the Terri Tyson story. I was hoping that the *Beacon* would put it all together for me.

Once I'd found the right year, it didn't take long to locate stories about Terri and Caleb. They had made the front page of the *Beacon* on and off for months. First there was coverage of the assault. Terri had been so badly beaten that she was in the hospital for months: in critical condition, then grave condition, then critical again. Then conscious, but brain-damaged. The fact that her injuries were so serious and so permanent accounted for the long sentence that the Crown had pushed for and received. It also explained why so many people thought that Caleb should have been charged with attempted murder.

Caleb had been identified as the prime suspect almost immediately. Terri's mother had returned from an afternoon bridge party. She'd heard a scream, recognized it as Terri's and rushed toward the sound. She'd found Terri lying on the patio behind the house and seen a man disappearing around the corner of the house next door. Mrs. Tyson had called 911 immediately. According to one article, Terri had regained consciousness briefly on the way to the hospital. The ambulance attendant had asked her if she knew who had done it. Terri had spoken one word — a name — before lapsing into unconsciousness. *Caleb.*

Mrs. Tyson had told the police that Terri had been acting strangely for the two days before she was attacked. "Something was bothering her," she'd said. Mrs. Tyson said she was sure that Terri had been planning to break up with Caleb. She and Terri had discussed it many times, although, under cross-examination at the trial, Mrs. Tyson had admitted that she was the one who had initiated these conversations, not Terri. When asked why she was so sure that Terri had been ready to go through with a break-up, Mrs. Tyson had answered, "Because Terri is a bright girl with a good future. I always knew it would be just a matter of time before she did the right thing." Mrs. Tyson said that she and Mr. Tyson had agreed that the right thing was accepting the university scholarship Terri had been offered.

The forensic evidence against Caleb was minimal. There were no footwear impressions on the Tysons' patio, on the patio next door or on the ground to match to Caleb's footwear. No fibres were located. No blood was found other than Terri's. Nothing useful was found under her fingernails — no blood or tissue from scratching or fending off her assailant.

Caleb's hands were bruised when the police found him and arrested him. He said that was because he'd "lost it" when he heard what had happened to Terri — he'd punched a tree. The crown attorney said he'd done that to cover the bruises he got from hitting Terri. There were no scratches or other marks on Caleb that suggested that someone — Terri — had struck out at him in self-defence. No one had seen Caleb or his bicycle. There were no bicycle tracks anywhere. There was just the fact that Terri was going to break up with Caleb — according to the Tysons — and that Caleb had made threats about what he would do if she did — again, according to the Tysons. Caleb's troubled history, the ambulance attendant's testimony about Terri's own last word, and Mrs. Tyson's account of Caleb's motive — coupled with one key piece of testimony — got Caleb convicted.

That testimony had come from Donald Brown. His account of what time it had been when Caleb got on his bicycle and rode away from his place established that Caleb had had the opportunity to assault Terri. It also demolished Caleb's alibi that he had been working at the Browns' until just minutes before the assault had happened and, therefore, couldn't possibly have made it to the Tysons' place and attacked Terri. To the jury, it caught Caleb in a lie.

Caleb's lawyer — Eric's uncle — had spent a lot of time cross-examining Mr. Brown. He had made a big deal of the fact that when the police had first asked Mr. Brown what time it was when Caleb had left his place, Mr. Brown had said he wasn't sure. But the next day he'd gone to the police and told them Caleb had left at six o'clock. He'd said he remembered it clearly. And nothing Eric's uncle could say or do had shaken his certainty on the witness stand.

Other witnesses were called — Jimmy Johnston and other townspeople I had never heard of or barely knew — who testified about incidents involving Caleb's explosive temper, his constant clashes with members of the Tyson family and his occasionally tumultuous relationship with Terri.

At the end of it all, Caleb had been found guilty. Too many people, it seemed, had too many negative things to say about him. And all the witnesses against him were upstanding, hard-working people who seemed above reproach.

Reading all of this so many years after the fact —
without having been involved, without even really
knowing all the parties — well, it made me wonder
how Caleb could have been convicted. Maybe that's
because when I think about the crimes that get
solved, I think about solid forensic evidence. But
Levesque is always saying that a lot of the time it's
not like on TV or in the movies. In a lot of crimes,
he says, it's not that simple.

In one issue of the paper, from before the trial
had even started, there was a small article about a
break and enter at the Darkes' house. The place
had been ripped apart. I remembered Ross telling
me that it had been trashed. Kyle's uncle Thaddeus was quoted as saying, "Well, I hope they found
whatever they were looking for." When pressed,
he'd said he had no idea what that was, but that
every drawer had been opened and emptied, every
closet turned upside down. "They must have been
looking for something," he said. "I hope they're
happy."

I removed the roll of microfilm from the microfilm reader, popped it back into its box, and sat
thinking. What if Caleb had been telling the truth?
I couldn't imagine how that would make a person
feel, especially after everything else that Caleb had
been through before that.

I stared at the blank screen of the microfilm
reader. Caleb Darke loved Terri Tyson. By all
accounts, including those of her own family, Terri

had loved Caleb. But in the two days before she was attacked, Terri had been acting strangely. She had left word for Caleb that she had something important to tell him. The Tysons claimed she'd been going to break up with him. But what if that wasn't what she'd been going to say? What if she had been going to tell him something else?

But what?

What could she have been intending to tell him?

If anyone knew for sure, it would have come out at the trial . . . wouldn't it?

Romeo and Juliet.

The Montagues and the Capulets.

The Tysons and the Darkes.

Daniel Tyson had wanted someone "better" than Caleb Darke for his daughter.

Charles Tyson had goaded Caleb into a fight. Charles Tyson had killed Caleb's grandfather in a hunting accident. And what had Ross told me about that? That Caleb was convinced that it hadn't been an accident. There had been a big investigation.

I thought back to the date I had read on the headstone in the cemetery. Matthew Sunday had died a few months before Terri Tyson was attacked. I fed the spool of microfilm into the reader again and cranked it until I found what I was looking for.

Man Killed in Hunting Accident.

The man was Matthew Sunday, 63, of East Hastings. He had been out in the woods about 60 kilometres northeast of East Hastings Provincial Park during the spring bear hunt. The man who had shot Matthew Sunday was Charles Tyson, 25, who was reported as "stricken" following the "terrible tragedy."

The story: Matthew Sunday's grandson, Caleb Darke, had driven him to the woods. Because of what had happened to Caleb's own father, he reportedly never went into the woods during hunting season without wearing a Day-Glo orange vest over his jacket. That must have been what Kyle had meant about Caleb wanting to be seen a mile away. Caleb had said that he'd dropped off his grandfather and arranged when and where to pick him up again. He had also told police that his grandfather had forgotten his vest, so Caleb had given the old man his own. He said he'd made his grandfather put it on before he left.

But Charles Tyson said that Matthew Sunday *hadn't* been wearing an orange vest. He'd said if Matthew had, he wouldn't have been shot in error. Charles's hunting companion also reported that there had been no orange vest. That companion was identified as James Johnston. Jimmy Johnston, I realized. Both men had told the police that they'd been appalled to discover Matthew Sunday, shot and fatally wounded. Jimmy Johnston had attempted first aid while Charles had gone for help. The vest — the "alleged" vest — had never been found.

There were a couple of follow-up articles. In one, Caleb claimed that the shooting had not been an accident, but he had nothing to back up his claim. Charles Tyson, for his part, claimed that Caleb had made up the story about giving his grandfather a Day-Glo orange vest, to try to make Charles look bad. The final article in the *Beacon* reported on the official finding of the coroner — that the shooting had been accidental, the old man mistaken for a bear.

* * *

I felt it as soon as I stepped through the main doors of the library and outside. It wasn't so much the number of people on the street — it was, after all, a warm spring Saturday afternoon. What alerted me that something had happened was the way the people were arranged on the street. No one was alone. Everyone was in a group of two or three or more. Everyone was talking.

My heart slammed to a halt in my chest. The first thing that occurred to me was *Levesque*. People were knotted together like that, leaning in toward each other like that, talking like that, because they had heard something about Levesque.

Something bad.

"Chloe?"

The voice sounded garbled. I felt something warm and hard in my hand and realized that I was gripping the iron railing that ran along the library steps.

"You don't look so good," the same voice said.

I didn't feel so good, either. My knees wobbled. My stomach churned.

"Chloe?"

I turned and focused hard. "I'm fine, Eric," I said.

"You heard the news?" His voice and his face were serious, but not sombre. He wasn't looking at me or talking to me the way he would be if something terrible had happened to Levesque.

"News?" I said.

"My uncle got Caleb released." He sounded proud.

"You mean, they don't think he shot Levesque?"

Eric's chest deflated a little. "He wasn't arrested for that. He was arrested for the assault on Jimmy Johnston," Eric said. "He's out on bail. But he's still a suspect in the shooting of your dad. Still, at least he isn't in custody. And at least he has a good lawyer." He peered at me again. "You sure you're okay?"

I told him again that I was fine. This time, I meant it.

* * *

Steve Denby looked like he hadn't slept in a month. But his extreme fatigue didn't seem to temper his exasperation at seeing me walk through the door.

"Don't start with me, Chloe," he said. He didn't just sound like Levesque; he sounded like Levesque on a bad day — grumpy and impatient. That brought me up short.

"Geez, Steve, I thought we were friends," I said. I really did. He had supper at our house at least every other week and he always kidded around with Phoebe and me.

"We are," he said. "But that's separate from this."

By *this* I knew he meant police work. Levesque had done a good job of indoctrinating him, but I knew how to score points too. First I sighed. Heavily. Then I made myself look serious and maybe even borderline-depressed. "How do you think I feel?" I said. "I mean, you're a cop, so maybe you're always expecting something like this to happen. But I'm not. Somebody shot him. You have no idea how much blood there was, Steve. I thought . . . " My lips quivered for real as I remembered how scared I had been. "I thought he was going to die." When I said that, a tear, a real tear, dribbled down my cheek.

Steve grabbed a tissue from a box on top of the filing cabinet behind him and thrust it at me. "He's going to be fine," he said. "I talked to the hospital about five times today already. They say he's doing just great."

"I want you to get whoever did it," I said.

He squeezed my shoulder. "I'm working on it."

"It wasn't Caleb."

He sank back down into his chair, his head ticking from side to side. "And that's based on what? The fact that Phoebe and Kyle are going together?"

Okay, so he was going to be like that. "I heard Caleb was released today," I said.

Steve's look was sharp.

"*Everyone* knows," I said. "Everyone's talking about it."

"Yeah, well, having a smart lawyer and being innocent are two different things," he said.

I hesitated, but said what I had to say anyway. "But you never charged him for the shooting."

Steve bristled. He shook his head. No charge meant that he didn't have enough evidence. At least, not yet. I decided to push a little, to see if Steve really was as hard as Levesque.

"I heard Caleb came in on his own," I said. "I heard that he said he wanted to talk to Levesque. You think he would have done that if he had just *shot* Levesque?"

The shadow of a smile rippled across Steve's lips.

"What?" I said.

"He's your step-father."

"Yeah? And?"

"So how come you call him by his last name?"

"Geez, Steve."

"Just asking."

"Why? So you can avoid answering my question?"

His smile evaporated. "Okay," he said. "Okay, so Caleb walked in here on his own. That's no big deal. Everyone knows he was wanted for questioning in conjunction with the stabbing of Jimmy Johnston."

"But if he'd shot Levesque — "

Steve shook his head again. Slowly. "I have the gun, Chloe," he said.

I waited. Nothing. Finally I had to ask. "Are you saying it's Caleb's gun?"

Steve hesitated. Then, "It was one of the rifles Jimmy reported stolen when he was" — here he paused — "attacked."

"Did you find Caleb's fingerprints on it?" I said.

Steve hesitated again, but finally shook his head.

"Where did you find it?" I said.

Nothing. He was being infuriatingly selective with the details he was willing to share.

"But why?" I said. "Why would Caleb shoot Levesque?"

"Who else would have wanted to, Chloe?"

"How about the Tysons?" I said. "How about Jimmy Johnston?"

"Why would they want to shoot him?"

I filled him in on my theory.

He looked doubtful, to say the least. "You're saying that maybe one of *them* shot the chief and that their plan was to make it look like Caleb did it, so that he'd be sent back to prison?"

I nodded.

"First of all, when you shoot someone, Chloe, you take a big chance you might kill them," Steve said. "Second, Daniel Tyson is being pretty effective at getting rid of Caleb without resorting to violence. He has the whole town stirred up. He's managed to get Caleb fired from his job and, as far as I know, no one else in town is willing to hire him. In a place like this, if you can keep up the pressure, you can drive someone out. You don't have to kill the chief of police. You just have to kill any chance Caleb has of leading a normal life here."

I hated to admit it, but that made sense.

He leaned farther back in his chair and rubbed his eyes, which made them redder than they already were and made him look more tired than he probably was.

"Caleb, though . . . " He sighed. "Caleb came back to town knowing he was in for a rough ride. He knew how the Tysons felt about him. He's made all the wrong moves since he got back. The guy has a history of making all the wrong moves, as far as I can tell. I've read his file, Chloe. It's a couple of inches thick. He hasn't exactly shown good judgment, let alone demonstrated any anger-management skills.

"I have to say, I feel sorry for the Tysons. I mean, he shows up just when Terri's starting to make a little progress. Her family's afraid his showing up is going to set her back." He shook his head. "I know Phoebe and Kyle are — well, whatever you call it these days. But facts are facts. After Caleb signed an undertaking to stay away from Terri, he broke it, at least according to Mrs. Tyson. He got into an argument with Jimmy and threatened him, in front of witnesses. Then he attacked him and stole some weapons."

"*Allegedly*," I said. "Levesque . . . " I had been going to say that Levesque wasn't convinced that Caleb had assaulted Jimmy Johnston. But Steve would wonder how I knew that.

"Caleb was already in big trouble," Steve said. "He'd been hiding out in the bush. He knew that if the chief found him, he'd bring him in. If the charges against him were proved, he'd be facing more jail time. And with his record . . . " He shrugged.

"He had the most to lose, Chloe."

"But he walked into the police station afterward."

"I'm not saying he's a cold-hearted killer," Steve said. "I'm just saying he's an impulsive guy with a quick temper who maybe doesn't think before he acts. Just like when he beat up Terri. I don't think he did that because he didn't love her. I think he did love her. I think he still does. But some people just let their emotions get the better of them. And if Caleb's record is anything to go by, he's one of those people."

I could see I was losing him. I had one last question. I wondered if he would answer it. "Steve?"

He greeted this with another sigh.

"Was Levesque here in the office when Phoebe called him from Kyle's place?"

Steve shook his head.

"Do you have any idea where he was?"

"He was out at Jimmy's place." This was news. "He said he wanted to follow up on the attack." Steve looked at me, his expression thoughtful.

CHAPTER SIXTEEN

I glanced at my watch. It had been a long day, and I had promised Phoebe that I'd be home for supper. But there was one more thing that was bothering me, one more thing that I wanted — *needed* — to do.

"Can you do me a favour, Steve?" I said.

From the pained expression on his face, you would have thought I was begging to practise dental surgery on him.

"I just want a lift somewhere," I said. He waited. "You know Mrs. Brown? She and her husband used to run a riding stable?"

Steve nodded, but his face was one hundred percent suspicion. "Why do you want to go out there?"

I could have told him it was none of his business, which was pretty much what he told me lately whenever I asked a question. But instead of revenge, I opted for virtue. I told him the truth — not exactly the *whole* truth, but nothing that was false, either. "She asked about Levesque at the hospital," I said. "I thought maybe I'd give her an update."

"Ever heard of the telephone?" Steve said.

"Ever heard of the personal touch?" I said.

Steve's suspicions hadn't eased a bit. "Eight years ago I wasn't much older than you are now," he said. "And I was living in North Bay, not here. But it made the papers there too. I remember reading about it. I used to read all the crime news. And

I remember that a Mr. Brown testified."

"Oh?" I said, fifty percent innocence and fifty percent Levesque — *I don't know anything, and even if I did, I'm not telling you.*

Steve sighed. "I guess I could run you out there," he said. "But I can't stay. You'll have to find your own way back."

"No problem," I said.

"You know," he said, "you really should get your driver's license."

"So I've been told."

Steve drove me to the Browns' house, which turned out to be located in, seemingly, the middle of nowhere. The house itself stood way back from the road. The expanse of lawn that surrounded it was bisected by fences, their white paint mostly peeled away. A couple of horses stood in a paddock near the house. Behind the house was a large stable, but I was willing to bet that few animals still called it home.

"You sure you're going to be okay?" Steve said as I opened the passenger door. "You're going to have to walk home."

It had taken us ten minutes to drive to the Browns' place from the centre of town, most of that at eighty kilometres an hour. I didn't need superior math skills to know that that translated into an awfully long walk home. And an awfully lonely one. On the drive out, we saw only one car — a grey four-door — and that was just as Steve was signalling to turn into Mrs. Brown's driveway.

I looked down at my shoes. They were sturdy and

comfortable. I walk more in one day in East Hastings than I ever did in a week back home in Montreal. "I can handle it," I said.

"I'll wait until she answers the door," he said.

"Steve," I said, turning his name into an expression of protest. What did he think I was, a helpless little kid?

"What if she's not home?" he said. "Do you want to walk all the way back to town if you don't have to?"

Okay, good point.

I climbed the porch steps and rang the doorbell. It took a minute, but finally I saw someone coming. Mrs. Amelia Brown opened the door. I glanced at Steve, who put the patrol car in reverse, executed a neat little turn and headed down the driveway toward the road.

Mrs. Brown studied me with lively grey eyes. "I know you," she said. "You're Chief Levesque's daughter."

"That's right," I said.

"How is he doing?"

I told her and she nodded. "It's a terrible thing," she said. "Imagine, shooting the chief of police! I don't think that's ever happened here before."

I didn't think it had ever happened in Toronto or Montreal or Vancouver, either.

"Can I talk to you about something, Mrs. Brown?" I said.

She nodded, but didn't ask what I wanted to talk about. She just smiled and invited me in. She led me to her kitchen — an enormous, sunny room at the back of the house, overlooking a gentle slope beyond which lay what looked like a pine forest.

"Can I offer you some lemonade?" she said.

I accepted and she poured us each a tall glass. She set out a plate of homemade cookies — peanut butter, chocolate chip and sugar cookies sprinkled with even more pink sugar.

"Mr. Brown had a sweet tooth," she said. "I can't seem to break the habit of baking regularly. Mostly I bake for the seniors club. The old folks like a fresh-baked treat."

They weren't the only ones. Her cookies were delicious.

"What can I do for you, dear?" she asked while I munched a sugar cookie.

"It's about Caleb Darke."

She sighed, but didn't seem surprised. It was almost as if she had expected to hear his name.

"I saw you in the parking lot when his bus arrived last week," I said. "Most people who turned up were there to tell him they didn't want him here. But you stayed on the sidelines."

She sipped her lemonade and said nothing.

"I saw you at the town meeting too," I said. "Everyone was yelling and screaming about Caleb. But you weren't."

Her grey eyes met mine, and still she waited.

I drew in a deep breath. "Mrs. Brown, Caleb said he was here chopping wood for your husband until six-thirty on the day Terri Tyson was attacked and beaten." I tried to gauge what she was thinking, but I couldn't. "Your husband said at the trial that Caleb left here at six o'clock. But at the trial, Caleb's lawyer said that *at first* your husband told the police he didn't know when Caleb left. He only remembered and told the police the next day."

"I don't know how I can help you," Mrs. Brown said. "I don't know when Caleb left. I wasn't here that day."

I had been reaching for another cookie, but now had no appetite for it. Why had I thought I was going to find out anything here?

"I was married to Donald for thirty-seven years," Mrs. Brown said. "We raised two children together. Two boys. I can't even begin to count how many horses we had over the years and how many children we taught to ride. I thought I knew everything there was to know about my husband. I thought there was nothing he could do that would surprise me."

I held my breath while I waited for her to say the one word I hoped she would say.

"But," she said — the magic word. "When you spend that much time with a man day in and day out, when you struggle to keep a business afloat and food on the table, when you sit up nights to talk about the kids, when you're young together and then you grow old together, you learn so much. You learn when the words 'don't worry' are genuine and when they're not."

She wasn't smiling any more. "Nine years ago, we were having trouble staying afloat. Business was falling off. I'm not sure why. Kids weren't as interested in horses and horseback riding as they used to be. I didn't know it at the time — I didn't know it until after Donald died a few years later — but he had gone to see Daniel Tyson and had taken a second mortgage on the place. After all those years, we were in debt again. We owed money to the bank. A lot of money."

To the bank. Daniel Tyson's bank.

Her eyes were clouded with sorrow and regret as they probed mine. "Donald liked Caleb," she said. "I know what they say about Caleb, and maybe some of it is true. He's a restless soul, or at least he was back then. Some people are. But when he said he would turn up to work, he turned up. And he worked hard. No one worked harder than Caleb, no matter how menial the chore. And I think even Donald saw the difference after Caleb started going with Terri. I know I saw it. Everything he did, Caleb did for Terri."

I clutched my nearly empty glass and waited.

"I don't know anything for sure," she said. "I never did. We never discussed it. He never wanted to talk about it. And I wasn't home that day. I was over in Elder Bay, visiting my niece who had just had a baby. I was there all day. I didn't get home until ten or eleven at night. So there are only three things I know for sure."

My mouth went dry. I gulped down a mouthful of lemonade.

"One," Mrs. Brown said, "Donald told me that

morning that Caleb was coming over to chop wood. Two, when we went to the hospital to see how Terri was, Donald had a long talk with Daniel Tyson. And three, right afterward, Donald went to talk to the police, and right after that, we got some relief from the bank. A loan that was coming due was extended — at very favourable terms. I had thought we were going to lose the place, but we didn't. Donald said it was because he had made a good case to Mr. Tyson down at the bank. But up until then, he had been pleading with Mr. Tyson and it hadn't done any good. Those three things I know. The rest I only feel."

She fell silent. For a minute, then two, then three, the only sound I heard was the tick-tick of the clock on the wall behind her.

Then Mrs. Brown sighed. "People who are — who aren't being entirely honest, can't seem to look you in the eye. Have you ever noticed that?" She shook her head. "Whenever Caleb's name came up after that, Donald looked somewhere else; he never looked at me. I must have asked him a hundred times, until he lost his temper and accused me of not believing him." She paused for a moment. "One time I threatened to go to the police. Donald was furious, but he told me to go ahead. He told me he'd just contradict what I said. And I couldn't prove anything. I still can't. It was just a feeling, you know? After Donald died, I did talk to the chief of police. I told him that I wasn't sure Donald had told the truth about exactly when Caleb had left. He said he'd look into it. But since Donald was dead, and there was no one who could say for sure that he was lying, or that Caleb hadn't left when Donald said he did, well, he wasn't sure he could do much. I think he talked to Daniel Tyson, but nothing came of it. And besides, by then Caleb had served two-thirds of his sentence and had been released from prison. He was living in Toronto, biding his time, I think, until he could come back home." She shook her head. "I don't know if Donald lied or not. I hate to say it, but I think he did. But there's nothing more I can do about it."

Well, that explained why she had never joined the get-Caleb-out-of-town movement. But it didn't help much — other than to make me *sure*, for the first time, that Caleb was an innocent man. And if he was innocent, then someone else was guilty. But who?

I thanked Mrs. Brown for her time, and started my long walk home. On the plus side, Mrs. Brown lives on the same side of town as me, which meant that if I kept up a good pace I'd be walking through my front door in a little over an hour.

I hiked down the driveway to the road, after which came the not-so-plus side. I had to climb a long, gentle, but relentlessly sloping hill. I like to think that I'm in pretty good shape, but that hill made me reassess my fitness level. I was sweating halfway up, and out of breath by the time I reached the top. But that wasn't the only reason — or even the real reason — why I stopped just at the top.

A grey car was pulled over at the side of the road, just beyond the rise of the hill. I was pretty sure it was the same grey car that I had seen drive by Mrs. Brown's house when Steve had dropped me off. At least, it looked like the same grey car. The hood was up now, as if the driver had run into engine trouble. But the driver wasn't bent over the engine. He wasn't even looking at it. Instead, he was standing straight up and it looked to me like he was watching the top of the hill. Only as I appeared did he peer down at the engine. Then he closed the hood.

I stayed at the top of the hill. I didn't want to look at him, but I couldn't take my eyes off him. It was a coincidence, right? At least, the first part had to be. It had to be a coincidence that Charles Tyson had driven by the Browns' house just as I arrived. Yet here he was, his car pointed in the opposite direction, just as I was leaving.

And, if it was a coincidence, why did I have that knot in my stomach? And why was I glued to this particular piece of gravel road? And why was I wishing that I didn't have to walk past Charles Tyson to get where I needed to go?

It's just Charles, I told myself. Good old Charles, who used to be a skinhead. Charles, who hated Caleb, partly because of who Caleb was and partly because of what Caleb had allegedly done. Charles, who'd been angry because Caleb had planned to marry his sister. Charles, who had tried to pick fights with Caleb time after time.

Charles, who had actually started a fight with Caleb, while Caleb had turned the other cheek.

I started down the slope toward him. He stood near the hood of his car until I was a few metres from his rear bumper. Then he came around to the driver's side and smiled at me.

"Hey, Chloe, what are you doing way out here?" he said.

Whatever else Charles Tyson was, he was my mother's boss. And that meant that it probably wasn't a good idea to say exactly what was flashing through my mind.

"Just walking," I said instead.

"Didn't I see you going into the Browns' house?" he said. Then, before I could answer, he said, "What happened to your police escort?"

What I did with my time was none of his business. I decided not to answer his questions. I also decided to walk around him.

He stepped out into the road to block my path. "Shirlene says you were at the store this morning," he said. "She says you came to drop off an envelope that your mother was supposed to have given me yesterday."

I tried again to circle him, but he stuck with me like a guard on a basketball court, doggedly blocking his player.

"Funny thing, though," he said. "I don't remember asking your mother for anything."

I flashed him my best hey-don't-ask-me-I'm-just-the-messenger look. "I guess you'll have to talk to Mom about that," I said.

He stepped a pace closer to me. Too close. I automatically retreated a pace.

"If I were you," he said, "I'd tell that sister of yours to stay away from Kyle Darke. Those Darkes are trouble."

I reminded myself again that he was my mom's boss. "I have to get home," I said, "before everyone starts worrying about me."

He nodded as if he understood completely. Then, as if the thought had just occurred to him, he said, "Except that your father's in the hospital and your mother's staying up there with him, isn't that right?"

"Excuse me, Mr. Tyson," I said. This time I darted around him and kept walking without looking back.

Behind me I heard a car door open and close and a car engine turn over. A moment later, Charles Tyson's grey car drew up alongside me. The passenger-side window was down. Charles looked over at me from the driver's seat.

"Come on," he said. "I'll give you a lift home."

"No, thanks," I said. I almost choked on the second word.

I glanced up ahead. The gravel road was empty as far as I could see. There was a house in the distance, but it was set as far back from the road as Mrs. Brown's. A little further on, a dirt road crossed the gravel road I was standing on now, but I didn't see anything up there, either.

"Come on, get in," Charles said. "It's a long walk home." His car crept along, keeping even with me.

"I'm fine, really," I said. "I need the exercise." *Go away,* I thought. *Go away now.*

He must have cranked the steering wheel to the right because his car swerved into my path, blocking my way. He got out from behind the wheel and slammed the door behind him. His face was red, his mouth jagged with rage. I glanced around frantically and saw a vehicle, a pickup truck, sliding along the dirt road toward the crossroads up ahead. I wondered if its driver would hear me if I yelled, but doubted it. The truck was too far away and, with my luck, the driver probably had his radio at full volume.

"Don't think I don't know what's going on here," Charles said. "Old Amelia is soft on Caleb, just like your old man. I wouldn't be surprised if she went to your father and told him what she told his predecessor. She thinks her husband lied about when Caleb left her place. Did she tell you that?"

I stared at him. I remembered seeing his car when Steve had driven me out here. I remembered that when Levesque was shot, Charles hadn't been in his store where he was supposed to be.

"Were you following me, Mr. Tyson?" I said. Had he been following Levesque on Friday?

"You people," he said with disgust. "You all think Caleb is innocent. You all think he did nothing. It doesn't matter that Terri identified him as her attacker."

Terri had said just one word — Caleb's name. It could have meant anything.

"You people think he didn't attack Jimmy, even though Jimmy says he did."

Charles knew that? Had Jimmy told him? If so, Jimmy must have known from Levesque's questions that Levesque had his doubts.

"You probably think he wasn't the one who shot your father too — even though the rifle that was used was one of the guns Caleb stole from Jimmy."

Charles knew an awful lot. Maybe too much.

"You can try to stir up trouble if you want to," Charles said, "but all that's going to happen is that your mother will end up out of work. So will your father. You understand me?" About halfway through his tirade he grabbed my arms and squeezed them hard. When I tried to break free, he started to shake me.

"Let me go," I said.

Instead, he tightened his grip. I was about to stomp down hard on his instep — a little trick Levesque had shown Phoebe, Brynn and me, back when we were still living in Montreal and he'd suddenly found himself step-father to three girls who insisted on going out after dark — when I heard the rumble of a badly muffled truck engine. Charles must have heard it too, because his hands fell away from my arms. We both turned toward the approaching truck, which slowed as it drew even with us. Caleb Darke peered out the driver's-side window. He and Charles locked eyes and, I swear, if either of them had been blessed with the type of telekinetic powers that you read about in horror novels, one of them would have burst into flames.

Then Caleb turned his black eyes on me. "You okay?" he said. Once again I was struck by the softness of his voice.

In fact, I was trembling. Charles had scared me. I scrambled away from him and darted across the road to Caleb's old truck. "Can you give me a lift?" I asked.

"You're crazy," Charles shouted at me. "You get in that truck with him and you're even crazier than he is."

I laid a hand on the hood of Caleb's truck for a moment to steady myself. Then I sucked in a deep breath and circled the truck. My hand was shaking when I gripped the passenger-door handle, but I managed to get the door open and to climb up onto the seat next to Caleb. He put the engine into gear, pulled up the road a few metres and turned the truck around.

"I'm sorry," I said.

He kept his eyes on the road. "What for?"

"For taking you out of your way. You were headed in the opposite direction."

"That's okay," he said. "Mrs. Brown won't mind if I'm late."

He was going to see Mrs. Brown? Charles was right — she did have a soft spot for Caleb.

"How's your father?" Caleb said.

"He's going to be okay."

I half-expected him to tell me that he hadn't done it, he hadn't shot Levesque. But he didn't. In fact, he didn't say anything. We drove in silence until I couldn't stand it anymore.

"Do you think Charles Tyson hates you enough to have shot my step-father?"

What Caleb did then was pretty much the last thing that I expected him to do. He smiled. And when he did, his whole face was transformed. He didn't look like the scary, sullen and possibly dangerous ex-convict that everyone — well, almost everyone — seemed keen to get rid of. Instead, he looked like just another easygoing guy.

At least he did until he said, "If someone shot your father, maybe someone had a problem with him, not me."

"Yeah, but you're the only person . . . " I swallowed the rest of my sentence. I had been going to say that Caleb was the only person who had a problem with Levesque, except that even I knew that wasn't true. The Tysons had a *big* problem with Levesque. Charles had just confirmed it for me. "What I meant was — "

"I know what you meant," Caleb said. "Did Charlie shoot the chief of police and fix it so everyone would think it was me? I don't know. It's really not my problem." He must have caught the look on my face because he added, "No offence."

Yeah. Well, none taken, I'm sure.

"As far as I know, you're the only suspect," I said. "No offence." And, yes, I put a little zing in the words.

He didn't say anything. He didn't even look at me.

We covered another kilometre or two in silence before turning up the road to my house. In another minute, he'd pull the truck over and I'd have to get out. It was now or never.

"Caleb?"

He glanced over at me.

"The Tysons are never going to let you get near her. You know that, right?"

That earned me another smile. He pulled over and idled the engine. When he looked at me again, his smile faded. "Someone hurt her bad," he said, "but it wasn't me. There are at least two people who know who really did it — Terri and whoever attacked her."

At least two people?

"Terri left a message for me the day before it happened," he said. "She told my uncle to tell me that she had to see me about something important. I was supposed to see her the next day, after she got off work. She said she'd meet me at her place as soon as she could get away from the camp."

"The camp?"

"Mr. Johnston's hunting camp," he said. "Terri was working there." Ross had mentioned that to me, but I'd forgotten. "So was Charlie. Mr. Johnston was expanding the place. He took on lots of help that year."

"The Tysons said that what she wanted to tell you was that she was breaking up with you," I said.

Caleb reached for me. At least, that's what I

thought he was doing and that's why I froze. He leaned toward me and one enormous hand reached for me and then over me. He wrenched the passenger-door handle.

"It's tricky to open from the inside," he said.

I unbuckled my seatbelt and jumped down to the ground.

"Mrs. Brown thinks her husband lied about when you left his place," I said.

Caleb's expression was sad and amused at the same time. "He did lie," he said. "I was there, remember?" He pulled the door closed, put the truck into gear and started back down the road.

As soon as I got into the house, I called the hospital and talked to Mom. Levesque had spent most of the day sleeping, she said. I asked her when she was coming home. Maybe tomorrow, she said. She asked how we were. Just fine, I assured her. I told her that we'd be back there first thing in the morning.

Phoebe came in with Kyle just as I was hanging up. Shendor awoke from her stupor in the corner of the kitchen and jumped up on Kyle, who greeted the dog's enthusiasm with good-natured attention. He bent down and scratched Shendor behind her ears and kissed her muzzle. Eeew!

"Kyle's staying for supper," Phoebe said. "We're celebrating. Caleb was released today."

"Yeah, I heard," I said. "You got a menu in mind?"

"We brought food," Kyle said. He gave Shendor another scratch, then got up and went into the front hall. He came back with two plastic bags from the grocery store in town. He set them onto the kitchen table and started unpacking them — chicken legs, mushrooms, green beans, potatoes, tomatoes, spinach.

I glanced at Phoebe, who shrugged. "It was Kyle's idea," she said.

Well, what do you know? All indications were that Kyle Darke knew his way around a kitchen. I decided to reserve judgment until dinner was actually on the table. I left him and Phoebe to it, promising I would clean up and do the dishes afterward.

Kyle not only knew a pot from a pan, but he could actually cook. He made chicken with mushroom sauce, fresh green beans, seasoned potato wedges, and a spinach and tomato salad.

"This is great, Kyle," I said for the tenth or eleventh time, while I was helping myself to seconds. Shendor was under the table, her head on my knees, mewling like a kitten. *Not a chance, doggie,* I thought.

I ate a little more chicken, then I said, "Hey, Kyle? How did Caleb and Terri get along?"

It was an innocent question. A well-intended question. After all, I was on Caleb's side and Kyle knew it. At least, I thought he did. So when I asked the question, I expected Kyle to be helpful.

Instead, his face went rigid. He set down his fork and stood up. "I don't want to talk about that," he said.

"Kyle." Phoebe stood up, too, and took him by the hand. By the way she glowered at me, you'd have thought I'd slapped him.

I talked fast — I had to so that he wouldn't break free of Phoebe's grip and flee, so that Phoebe wouldn't give in and flee with him.

"Kyle, look, this is important, so hear me out, will you? According to Mr. Brown, Caleb left his place because Terri wanted to tell him something important. Mrs. Tyson said Terri was going to break up with him. You said Terri was at your house almost every day. You saw them together. Do you think it was *true*? Were they going to break up?"

Kyle's fists were clenched at his sides. His face was red. His eyes burned. "Everyone's right about you," he said. "You're always sticking your nose into other people's business."

Sticking my nose into other people's business? Even Phoebe looked a little stunned at that.

"Chloe's just trying to help Caleb," she said. "You said yourself he would never hurt my dad. And if he loved Terri he wouldn't hurt her, either. So . . . " She broke off, her attention snagged by a movement of Kyle's head — a twitch that seemed to change entirely the set of his face. He was still angry. I could see that from the white of his knuckles. He was angry and tense and . . . something else. Something that Phoebe seemed to have a better fix on than I did.

"Kyle?" she said. She spoke as softly as a mother cooing at her baby. She moved toward him in slow motion, a wrangler approaching a wild pony. "Kyle, what's the matter?"

When Kyle turned his back on her, Phoebe reacted as if he'd slammed a door in her face. She looked at me — stung, confused, fighting back tears.

I shook my head. He was *her* boyfriend. Then I felt sorry for her. I nodded at her, encouraging her.

"Kyle?" she said again, and touched his arm.

Kyle spun around so abruptly that I caught my breath. His face was so twisted, so tortured, that all I could think was, *He's going to hit her.*

But he didn't.

"He did it," Kyle said instead.

Phoebe did the same thing I did. She frowned and shook her head, as if she were trying to clear her ears. We exchanged glances.

"Who — ?" she began.

"Caleb," Kyle said. "He did it. He hurt Terri and it's all my fault."

"What?" Phoebe said. She stared at him as if he'd suddenly switched from English to Latin.

Kyle's face was a study in agony.

"Kyle," Phoebe said, "what's the matter?"

He looked at her, then at me, then at her again.

"It's my fault," he said. He was focused on the table now, and his voice was a strangled whisper. "I should never have told him."

"Told him what?" Phoebe said. She inched closer to him.

"I saw her," he said.

"Terri?"

He nodded. "I saw her out at the cabin." He raised his head then and looked at me, not Phoebe. "My grandfather was shot," he said. Explaining.

"She knows," Phoebe said. "I told her."

"Charles Tyson shot him," I said, repeating what I had been told and what I had read in the newspaper. "Charles said it was an accident. Caleb said he did it on purpose."

"Charles lied," Kyle said. "Terri knew he'd lied."

Terri *knew* he'd lied? "She told you that?" I said.

Kyle shook his head. Phoebe squeezed his arm. He turned and looked into her eyes. Then he took one of her hands into his.

"I was out at the cabin," he said. "I was just fooling around, you know. I used to hang out there all the time before Caleb and Terri started to fix the place up. Then one time I messed up some fresh paint, and Caleb told me not to go out there anymore. He told me the place was off limits to me. So I started sneaking out there instead."

A real Darke, I thought. *Tell them no and they just find a way around it.*

His head was bowed as he spoke. Phoebe held tightly to his hand.

"I was out there the afternoon before," he said.

"Before?" Phoebe said.

"The afternoon before Terri . . ." His voice trailed off. He drew in a deep breath. "Caleb was up north. He wasn't going to be back until after supper time. So I figured no one would catch me out there. The cabin has a loft. From up there, you can look down into almost the whole place. I used to love to play up there.

"I was there when Terri came in. I hid. I didn't want her to see me, because I wasn't supposed to be there. I didn't want her to tell Caleb. He'd get mad. Anyway, I saw her come in. She just sat there for a while, at the table. Then she lit the stove."

"Gas?" Phoebe said.

"Wood," Kyle said. "I thought she was going to make some tea. Terri was very big on tea. Then I saw her take something out of her backpack. A package, wrapped in brown paper. She unwrapped it. I saw right away what it was. That's when I knew *she* knew."

"What was it?" Phoebe said.

"Caleb's vest," Kyle said. "I saw his initials on it."

Phoebe's expression was blank as she waited for more. When Kyle didn't continue, she glanced at me.

I filled her in. "Caleb's hunting vest. He said he made his grandfather put on an orange vest when he took him into the woods," I said. "But Charles said that Matthew Sunday *hadn't* been wearing a vest. He said that's how he shot him by accident. The vest was never found."

"So how did Terri end up with it?" Phoebe asked.

"And what was she doing with it out at the cabin?" I said.

"Burning it," Kyle said.

"What?"

"She lit the stove. She came out there to burn it."

"You saw her do that?"

"I saw her put it on the table near the stove. Then I — I knocked into something and I had to duck down so she wouldn't see me. But I stayed down for only a few seconds. A minute at the most. And when I looked again, the vest was gone and Terri was poking at the stove."

"I don't get it," Phoebe said. "Why would Terri burn Caleb's vest?"

"The vest could prove that Charles was lying," I said.

"*Could* prove?" Phoebe said.

"If Kyle's grandfather was wearing it when he was shot," I said, "there'd be a bullet hole in it. It would prove that the shooting didn't happen the way Charles said it did. Bears don't wear Day-Glo orange vests."

Phoebe frowned. "But why would Charles lie?"

Kyle stared at her. Stared at her and waited until Phoebe's eyes widened and her mouth formed a little circle and she said, "Oh." Her hand went to her mouth. She started to shake her head. "Oh, you don't think — "

"He did it on purpose," Kyle said. "He probably thought it was Caleb. And Terri knew. She had the vest. She had the proof. And she burned it. And . . . " He looked down at the table again. "And I told Caleb."

"Oh," Phoebe said again, a little quicker this time.

"And you think that because of that . . . " I said.

"He told me not to tell anyone," Kyle said.

Phoebe shook her head. "But why not? Especially

if it showed that Charles had been lying?"

Kyle looked lost. "He told me not to tell anyone what I had told him — and after what happened to Terri . . . "

"You were just trying to help him again," I said.

"But he could have proved that Charles was lying," Phoebe said.

"Terri made sure he couldn't," Kyle said. "She burned the vest. I looked in the stove after she left and it wasn't there. It wasn't anywhere."

"Without the vest, it would have been just like before," I said. "It would have been Caleb's word against Charles's." Except for one thing. "Tell me again when you saw her, Kyle."

He told me.

"And when did you tell Caleb?"

"I didn't get a chance until the next morning. His car broke down. He had to hitchhike home. He must have got back in the middle of the night because he was there when I got up. He was just leaving to go to the Browns'. That's when I told him."

"What did he say?"

Kyle shook his head slowly. "That's the thing. He didn't say anything except okay."

"Okay?" Phoebe said.

Kyle nodded. "He said okay. He made me promise not to tell anyone. Then he left for the Browns'."

"I thought Terri had called him and said she wanted to see him," I said. "Caleb told Mr. Brown that he was going to meet her after work. Mr. Brown said he'd seemed upset."

"No wonder," Phoebe said.

"She did call. She called that day, before Caleb was back from up north," Kyle said. "She left a message with Uncle Thad. She said to tell Caleb she wanted to see him after she got off work the next day."

"So maybe it was true," Phoebe said. "If she did what Kyle said she did, then she must not have loved him. She must have been going to break up with him."

Kyle hung his head for a moment. Then he looked back up at her. "I don't think he would shoot your father," he said. "I really don't. But the thing with Terri . . ."

She hugged him. My little sister threw herself at Kyle, wrapped her arms around him and hugged him.

I left them to it. I had a phone call to make. To Ross. When I was done I went to find Kyle and Phoebe again.

"So, Kyle," I said, "where exactly is your grandfather's place?"

Phoebe's eyes narrowed. "Why?"

"Just an idea," I said. "Probably a crazy one." That's what I said. It wasn't what I hoped, though.

CHAPTER SEVENTEEN

I was up before Phoebe, gulping coffee and checking the map that I had asked Kyle to draw for me. My plan was to pay a visit to Matthew Sunday's old cabin, then meet up with Ross down by the highway so that he could drive Phoebe and me to the hospital. I left a note for Phoebe, shouldered my backpack, and headed out.

The whole way there, I was hoping. Hoping and telling myself not to be so ridiculous. Hoping and telling myself that it wasn't going to happen, that I wasn't going to find it. Because that's the way things turn out in real life, right?

Like the time when Brynn, my older sister, was in third grade and begged to wear her friend Sarah's ring. It was a real gold ring. And Sarah finally said yes, and Brynn slipped it on her finger before the two of them went out to the playground to skip or play tag or play on the climber or whatever they were doing. It wasn't until after they had gone back into the classroom that Brynn noticed that the ring wasn't on her finger anymore. And it wasn't until after she made this discovery that Sarah told her — almost hysterically — that the ring had been a gift from her grandmother just before she'd died and that it was very, very valuable. Which of course made Brynn cry. So, after school, she and I combed every inch of the schoolyard for that ring. The whole time we were looking, I pictured myself finding it. Finding it and being a hero — even though maybe a thousand kids, and who knew how many passersby, had trooped through the schoolyard in the meantime. I kept hoping. Because I really wanted to be the one to find it. I wanted to save the day.

Just like now. I think I knew my chances weren't good. I think that's why I didn't tell Kyle or Phoebe exactly why I was going out there.

Kyle's map was bang-on accurate. I found the cabin without any trouble. It was made of logs and set in a clearing that looked like it hadn't been properly tended in years. It was weedy and over-grown with seedlings that were rapidly turning into saplings.

I picked my way through the scrub and peeked through a dusty window. The place looked deserted. I climbed the few rickety steps to the door and tried the knob. It gave. The cabin wasn't even locked. But then, it wasn't exactly on the beaten path. Either that or — the thought occurred to me just as I was pushing the door open — Caleb was here again. Kyle had said that he'd been out here a lot since he was released. I decided to play it safe. I knocked on the door. There was no answer. I drew in a deep breath and pushed open the door.

The cabin was sparsely furnished — a sofa and a couple of chairs just inside the front door; a kitchen table and chairs in the back, in what I took to be the kitchen area; a bed, a dresser and a bedside table visible through another door to my left. And although the place had looked neglected from the outside, the kitchen table sparkled in the streaky sunlight, as did the small expanse of kitchen counter. Someone had been here recently. A steep set of stairs led to a small loft over the living room. From up there, a person would have a perfect view of the kitchen and the big wood stove.

Now that I was here, I wasn't sure where to begin.

I started toward the bedroom to have a closer look around. I was halfway there when I heard a door click shut behind me. I whirled around, my heart pounding in my chest.

It was Caleb.

He loomed in front of the closed door, blocking my exit, staring at me with night-dark eyes. "What are you doing here?" he said.

"I — " I what? I decided to walk into a place that doesn't belong to me because I decided to snoop around, but, hey, it's okay because I'm doing this all for you? "Kyle told me that Terri was here the day before she was attacked," I said. "He told me about the vest."

Surprise replaced the unreadable expression on his face, but he said nothing.

"He told me what he saw," I said. "He said he told you."

Caleb stiffened. His face became rigid and hard. "Yeah, well, I've done my time," he said, "so I don't care what you think. I don't care what anyone thinks."

"You care what *Kyle* thinks, don't you?"

That earned me another dark, silent look.

"Kyle thinks you did it," I said. "And he thinks it's his fault. He thinks that if he hadn't told you he saw Terri destroy the vest, none of this would have happened."

Caleb blinked. Then he stared at me. It took him forever to say, "Kyle thinks I did that to Terri?"

"He feels responsible," I said. "He thinks she chose to protect Charles and to lie to you. And because he saw, and because he told you — "

"I love Terri," he said. Love, not *loved*. "I don't know why she did what she did. I never got a chance to ask her. It's one of the reasons I wanted to see her when I got out. I wanted to see if she could tell me why she did it. But I loved her then and I love her now. I'd never hurt her."

"She didn't do it," I said.

Caleb didn't seem to register my words.

"She didn't burn the vest," I said.

"But Kyle — "

"Kyle *assumed*. He didn't actually see her do it. But I know for a fact that she still had it in her backpack that night." I explained what Ross had told me — how she'd gone to answer the phone while she was baby-sitting him that night, after she had visited the cabin. I explained that Ross had snooped in her backpack and had seen what he thought was a jacket wrapped in brown paper. "It was orange," I said. I had quizzed Ross about it just last night.

"She *didn't burn it*, Caleb," I told him. "She still *had* it. I think she was planning to show it to you after you got back to town. But you weren't expected until late that night, and when your car broke down you were even later, so she had to wait until the next day. But before she could meet you, someone stopped her."

Caleb's look was long and silent and impossible to read. Finally he said, "Then it's still gone. Whoever attacked her . . . " And he was probably thinking the same thing I was; he was probably thinking, *Charles*. "He must have taken it and destroyed it."

"I don't think so," I said.

He shook his head slowly.

"Your house was trashed after you were arrested, right?" I said. "I saw an article in the newspaper. Your uncle was interviewed."

"Yeah," he said. "So?" Then the lights came on behind his eyes. "You think someone was looking for the vest."

I nodded. Terri had had the vest when she was at Ross's house. She'd probably been hoping to show Caleb that night. But she couldn't. He wasn't back. And she couldn't have had it with her when she was attacked. If she had, why would anyone have bothered to search Caleb's house afterward? Nor could she have hidden it at her house. That's the first place Charles would have looked. If it had been there, he would have found it and destroyed it. So again, why search Caleb's house? "Whoever tore your house apart probably relaxed later, when you didn't produce it. You didn't even bring it up when you were arrested, did you?"

"What would have been the point?" he said. "I thought it didn't exist anymore. And they thought I did that to her because she was breaking up with me. You have any idea what they would have thought if they knew about the vest — if they knew *I* knew about it, and I knew she had burned it?"

"Terri sounds like she was really smart," I said. "Smart enough that when you didn't come home when you were supposed to, she might have hidden it for safe-keeping. You have any idea where she would hide something that valuable — something she didn't want anyone to find?"

Caleb turned his head away from me. At first I thought that was his way of dismissing me. Out of sight, out of mind. But then I saw that he was looking through a window that faced the area behind the cabin. "She wasn't home that morning," he said. She. *Terri*. "I stopped to call her on my way to the Browns'. Her mother said she'd already left, but she wasn't at work, either. I called there."

A hand went to a pocket in his pants. He pulled out a key ring and walked through the kitchen area. He opened the back door and stepped outside. I followed him, through the scrubby backyard and into the trees to a small shed. I turned and looked back. I couldn't see the cabin through the trees, which meant that from the cabin, this shed was probably invisible. When I turned back, Caleb was unlocking a sturdy padlock on the door.

I joined him as he pushed open the door and we looked into the dark little shed. It took a moment for my eyes to adjust. The place was filled with neatly arranged gear — tools and a small tool bench along one wall. Traps hung on another. There were more traps against a third wall — that was the pile of gear Caleb was looking at. Traps piled on a big wooden box. Caleb ducked inside and started removing them from the top of the box, one by one. Then, hands trembling, he lifted the lid.

I didn't know which of the emotions I felt then was strongest — surprise or disappointment. The box was filled with household things — packages of sheets and pillowcases, a four-setting package of dishes, an eight-setting package of kitchen cutlery, dishtowels, blankets. They were all the things a person would need to stock a house or apartment, and all of it was in its original packaging. Most of the packages had the price tags still attached.

"Terri bought all of this," Caleb said, lifting out a plastic-wrapped blanket. It was buttery yellow. "It was supposed to be for us," he said.

In the distance, I heard a car engine. Caleb must have heard it too, because he turned his head. Then someone called his name.

"I'll be back," he said.

I didn't even watch him go. I was looking at that box, and thinking. Thinking about where I'd hide something if I were Terri. I started lifting things out — dishes, cutlery, a frying pan, some pots —

until almost everything was stacked neatly on the floor at my feet. Everything except a brown paper bag that had been flattened under all that stuff. I plucked it out of the trunk. The paper crinkled in my hand. There was something inside. Something soft and supple.

I held my breath as I opened the bag and pulled out a bright orange vest with the initials C. D. stencilled on the back. There was a dark brown stain on it. And a hole — a bullet hole — through it. I stared at it, trying to think. I folded it as carefully as I could with shaking hands, and tucked it back into the brown paper bag. Then, feeling like a big hero — like Superman or Wonder Woman — I ran to find Caleb.

He wasn't alone. Jimmy Johnston and Charles Tyson were with him. They were standing near a blue van with tinted windows that was parked in front of the cabin. But that wasn't what killed my enthusiasm and brought me up short. What ground me to a halt — what made my pulse race and my mouth go dry — was the fact that Caleb's hands were up in the air. What seemed to have sent them there was the rifle that Charles was pointing directly at Caleb.

All three of them heard me. All three turned to look at me. Two of them seemed stunned by my sudden appearance. It was Caleb who spoke to me first. One word.

"Run!"

"Grab her, Jimmy," Charles said, without lowering his rifle even a millimetre, without taking his eyes off Caleb.

I bolted — about a metre — before a hand clamped around my arm and hauled me back to where the others were standing.

"Let her go," someone said. I turned and saw Daniel Tyson emerge from the van. "For heaven's sake, let her go."

Charles didn't flinch from his target. "It's too late now, Dad. She's here. She's seen."

My head was spinning. What was happening? What were they all doing here?

"Charles, she's just a kid," Daniel Tyson said. "Her father — "

"You want to get rid of him, don't you?" Charles said. I wasn't sure who he was talking to — his father or Jimmy Johnston. Maybe both. "This can still work," he said. "Dad, go through his pockets. Get his keys."

Daniel Tyson stayed where he was.

"We go with the same plan," Charles said. "We take Terri up to the lake, just like we planned." Terri? I glanced at the van. Was Terri in there? "Caleb shows up. He tries to get at her and we stop him."

"But the girl — " Daniel Tyson said. He meant me.

"The girl happened by. She tried to protect Terri. Caleb killed her. We had to shoot him."

My knees turned to water. This couldn't be happening. I couldn't possibly have heard what I thought I had just heard. If Jimmy Johnston hadn't been holding my arm, I would have collapsed for sure.

"Killed her?" Daniel Tyson said. His voice was high, panicky. "Nobody said anything about killing anyone. We were just going to catch him trying to get to Terri again."

"We're in this now," Charles said. "If we let her go, what do you think she's going to do? And anyway, if Caleb gets near Terri, what's the worst that's going to happen to him? He's going to get his wrist slapped. Maybe he'll do a little time. But he'll be back, Dad. He's never going to leave her be. Are you?" he said, spitting the words at Caleb.

Caleb stood in front of Charles Tyson, his hands up, his eyes blank.

"You know what he did to Terri," Charles said. "You think he should be able to just walk away?"

Mr. Tyson glanced back over his shoulder into the van. Then he looked at me. I've never seen such sadness on a man's face. His shoulders slumped as he started toward Caleb. Watching him, knowing what he was going to do, made me find my voice.

"Terri knew that Matthew Sunday's death wasn't an accident," I said. "She had proof. Is that why you did it, Charles? Is that why you attacked your own sister? Because she was going to the police?"

Three pairs of eyes turned to look at me — Charles's, Jimmy Johnston's and Mr. Tyson's. But only one of them looked surprised, and it wasn't the one I had expected.

"What are you talking about?" Charles said. Charles Tyson — manager of the East Hastings

Canadian Tire and my mother's boss. A man with a killer secret.

"The vest," I said. "The vest that Matthew Sunday was wearing when you shot him. Terri found it. And you knew, didn't you?"

A bunch of things happened all at once. When I thought about it all later, it was like I was looking at a series of snapshots. Snapshot number one: Mr. Tyson and Charles, both staring open-mouthed at Jimmy Johnston. Snapshot number two: Jimmy, his grip still firm on me, shaking his head in denial. Snapshot number three: Jimmy Johnston zeroing in on the bag I was carrying, interested in it now, reaching for it. Snapshot number four: Caleb, taking advantage of the fact that everyone was looking at me — or were the Tysons looking at Jimmy Johnston? — and reaching for the barrel of the rifle Charles had aimed at him. Caleb grasping it, wrenching it from Charles and, in one fluid movement, spinning it so that now it was pointed at Charles.

"Let her go, Mr. Johnston," he said, his voice soft but firm, calling him Mr. Johnston even now.

Jimmy Johnston did the direct opposite. He tightened his grip on me, to the point where I thought he was going to cut off the circulation to my left arm, and pulled me close to him too, so that I was right in front of him, shielding him. Then he dragged me back toward the van.

"I'm warning you, Mr. Johnston," Caleb said. "Let her go."

"Or what?" Jimmy said. "Or you'll shoot Charles? Go ahead. See how that improves your situation." He yanked me back until we were beside the front passenger-side door. I glanced inside. I saw another rifle on the floor in front of the seat and, in the back, Terri in her wheelchair. My eyes shifted back to the rifle. If Jimmy got hold of it . . .

I did the only thing I could think of. I stomped down hard on his instep. When he yowled with pain, I wrenched free of him.

"There's another gun in the van," I called to Caleb.

A hand clamped around my arm again. Jimmy Johnston, his face contorted with pain and rage, groped for the bag that I held in my right hand. If he got the vest away from me and if he got away from Caleb . . . I yanked my arm up, up, up and flung the bag over the top of the van to Caleb.

Daniel Tyson intercepted it. I scrambled around the front of the van, as far from Jimmy Johnston as I could get.

"Caleb, he's going to — "

Mr. Tyson reached into the bag and pulled out the orange vest. He turned it over and over in his hands, studying it. He looked at his son. Then he turned to Jimmy. His face was flooded with confusion and something else. He looked like a man who had been groping in a dark room that was suddenly flooded with light. "Terri had this?" he said.

"Yes," I said. "She hid it. She was going to tell Caleb about it, and I think they were going to go to the police. But someone attacked her before she could."

Mr. Tyson fingered the vest in silence. He looked at Jimmy Johnston.

"How did she get this?" he said. "I thought you'd destroyed it. Isn't that what you promised?"

Now I felt like *I'd* just stepped into the light. The vest was proof positive that Charles had lied about mistaking Matthew Sunday for a bear. But it *wasn't* news to Daniel Tyson, I realized. He'd known about it all along. He thought that it had been destroyed. He wasn't shocked that the vest *existed*. He was shocked by the fact that *Terri* had found out about it.

Charles looked as surprised to see the vest as his father did. Had he too assumed it had been destroyed?

But it hadn't been. Terri had found it. She had taken it from the one person who had known it still existed: Jimmy Johnston, the person who had apparently promised Mr. Tyson that he would destroy it. But he *hadn't* destroyed it. He had held onto it. *Why*?

I could think of only one reason. "Was Mr. Johnston blackmailing you, Mr. Tyson?" I said.

I guess I was surprised that Mr. Tyson didn't deny it. Then I remembered something Levesque had told me once. Most people — people who aren't complete psychopaths — are actually relieved when they get found out and the whole thing is over. They're glad to be finished with all the hiding, the pretending and lying.

"You said you'd gotten rid of it," Mr. Tyson said to Jimmy. "You said that was the end of it." He looked at his son. "Did you know?"

Charles was staring at the vest, confused.

"Did you know that Terri had this?" Daniel Tyson said.

Charles was shaking his head before the one word left his mouth. "No."

Mr. Tyson turned his back to Caleb. "Don't lie to me, son," he said.

"I swear," Charles said, "I didn't know."

Mr. Tyson then turned to Jimmy Johnston. "Tell me it wasn't you, Jimmy," he said.

Jimmy's smile was twitchy. "Hey, Danny, you know *me*," he said.

Mr. Tyson edged closer to the van. It was as if he had forgotten that Caleb was still there. He grabbed hold of the driver's-side door handle, yanked the door open and dove inside. Jimmy started for the passenger door, but a warning from Caleb stopped him in his tracks. When Mr. Tyson straightened up again, he was holding a rifle. He pointed it at Jimmy.

"Geez, Danny," Jimmy said. He thrust his hands up into the air. "Take it easy, will you?"

"*You* beat my Terri, didn't you?" Mr. Tyson said. "You did this to her." He raised the rifle and sighted down it.

"Caleb," I said. But Caleb wasn't moving, either.

A shot ripped through the air. I've been to plenty of movies and heard plenty of gunshots in full

Dolby, but none of them even came close to the sound of Mr. Tyson's rifle. Someone yowled. It came from inside the van. *Terri*, I thought.

Caleb glanced at the van and took a step toward it, then stopped again and held his ground. Jimmy Johnston's face went as white as milk. He was bent in a cringe when I looked at him and it seemed to take him forever to straighten up again. When he did, he looked himself over and seemed surprised to find that he was okay.

"Tell me exactly what happened or, I swear, I won't miss next time," Mr. Tyson said.

Silence from Jimmy. Mr. Tyson raised his rifle again.

"Geez, Danny," Jimmy said. "Okay. Okay. The truth is, I don't even know how she got hold of it. She must have got into the safe when I wasn't looking — "

"Or maybe you left it open," Charles said. "It wouldn't have been the first time."

"Let him tell it, Charles," Mr. Tyson said. He wagged the rifle barrel at Jimmy.

"All I know is, I had it locked up and then it was gone and she was the last person who had been in the office. So I went looking for her to ask her about it. You know what she said?"

Mr. Tyson was staring at him. He didn't say a word.

"She said she was going to go to the cops," Jimmy said. "She was going to give them the vest. She said she was through with you and Charles telling her what to do and that she was going to make sure you couldn't do that anymore. You didn't want that, did you, Danny? You didn't want her ending up with the likes of him, did you?"

Mr. Tyson didn't move, didn't answer.

"I tried to reason with her, but she wouldn't listen. She was going to go to the police. She didn't care what it would do to Charles or you."

"Me?" Mr. Tyson blinked. "You're telling me you attacked my daughter as a *favour* to *me*?"

Jimmy raised his trembling hands a little higher, as if that might save him.

"You sure you weren't protecting yourself, Jimmy? What would the police make of what you did? Aiding and abetting after the fact? Conspiracy to conceal a crime, likely. Blackmail."

"Dad, please . . . "

Mr. Tyson ignored his son.

"Danny, please, I didn't mean to hurt her," Jimmy said. "I swear. I was just trying to stop her from doing something stupid and, I don't know, she hit me and I lost my temper . . . " He shrugged helplessly.

I glanced at Caleb.

Caleb kept his rifle in a tight grip, but it wasn't aimed at Charles anymore. He had changed position, and now it was aiming at Jimmy Johnston. Caleb, who didn't like guns, was sighting down the barrel. His hand trembled. I watched as he steadied himself.

"Caleb," I said. "He's unarmed."

Jimmy Johnston had his hands in the air. His eyes were staring at the barrel of the rifle in Caleb's hands.

I groped in my backpack for my cell phone.

"I'm going to call Steve Denby," I said.

Charles Tyson spun around to face me. I shrunk back, afraid of what he might do.

But Mr. Tyson lowered his own weapon and laid a hand on his son's arm. "We have to finish this," he said. "It's time to put this right." Then he nodded at me.

I punched in the number for the East Hastings Police Department. My fingers were trembling so badly that I had to dial twice before I got through.

"Steve?" I said. "It's Chloe."

Caleb lowered his own weapon. Then he handed it to Daniel Tyson and climbed into the back of the van. I heard his voice, sweet and low, talking to Terri, telling her everything was okay.

CHAPTER EIGHTEEN

Mom shook her head again. She was sitting on a chair next to Levesque's bed, trying to follow what we were saying. Levesque was propped up on a couple of pillows. He wasn't as pale as he'd been the last time I had seen him. He looked tired, but alert. Steve Denby had pulled up a chair and sat down. I was perched on the windowsill. Phoebe was standing just inside the door with Kyle.

"So it was Jimmy Johnston who attacked Terri?" Mom said.

Steve nodded. "Jimmy has refused to answer any questions. So has Charles. But from what we've been able to piece together, it looks like Charles saw Caleb and his grandfather heading into the woods. Caleb was wearing his vest, the way he always did. Charles must have let them get far enough ahead that he wouldn't be seen. He tracked what he figured was still both of them, and shot at what he thought was Caleb. But it *wasn't* Caleb. It was his grandfather."

"Because Caleb had left by then. And he'd given his grandfather the vest," I said.

Steve nodded. "He tried to claim it was an accident, but Jimmy knew it wasn't. He was there the whole time. He saw it. But he agreed to help Charles. He sent Charles to get help. Then he took the vest off Matthew Sunday. He removed his jacket and his shirt, too. He said he was trying to give him first aid — but, if you ask me, he removed those items to muddy the waters."

"Huh?" Mom said.

Levesque squeezed her hand. "If he'd taken off just the vest, whoever investigated the shooting might have noticed some inconsistencies in blood patterns," he said. "By removing several layers of clothing, Jimmy altered the crime scene. That made it harder for an investigator to see what had really happened."

Mom nodded.

"Jimmy backed up Charles's story," Steve said. "He kept the vest and used it to persuade Daniel Tyson to arrange a low-interest bank loan so that he could expand his hunting camp. He also persuaded Tyson to invest some of his own money into the place. Then Terri got hold of the vest. We'll never really know how. She must have realized right away what it was. She called Caleb and arranged to meet him. But Jimmy got to her first."

"Who knows what might have happened if Mrs. Tyson hadn't arrived home when she did that night," Levesque said.

"Jimmy heard her coming and fled," Steve said.

"And when the ambulance attendant asked Terri who had attacked her, Terri said Caleb's name," I said. "But she didn't mean that Caleb had *hurt* her."

Steve shook his head. "The ambulance attendant assumed," he said. "An honest mistake."

"And Daniel Tyson was so sure it was Caleb who

had hurt Terri, he tried to make sure the charge stuck by getting Mr. Brown to lie about what time it was when Caleb left his place," I said.

"That's the one thing Mr. Tyson has talked about," Steve said. "He claims that Mr. Brown approached *him* and said maybe he was mistaken when he told the police that Caleb had left his place at six. Mr. Tyson says he approved Brown's loan out of gratitude, but he claims he didn't bribe Brown into perjury. With Brown dead, there's no one to contradict him. No matter how you look at it, though, Caleb was sentenced to eight years for a crime he didn't commit."

"That's awful," Phoebe said. She was clinging to Kyle's hand. Kyle looked down at the floor. He didn't say anything. Neither did anyone else. No words, it seemed, could even come close to expressing the injustice that Caleb had suffered.

"But who shot you, Louis?" Mom said. "And why?"

"It was Jimmy Johnston, wasn't it?" I said. "You were out at *his* place when Phoebe called you. You didn't believe that Caleb had attacked him, did you?"

Levesque shook his head. "It just didn't make sense," he said. "All Caleb wanted was to be with Terri. Why would he attack Jimmy and steal weapons from him? And even if he did assault Jimmy, why stab him? And with what? Jimmy said it was a knife, but he couldn't describe it. That's why I went out there again — to ask Jimmy a few more questions."

"You think the wound was self-inflicted?" Mom said.

"It crossed my mind," Levesque said.

"And when I called you from Kyle's place, you told me to stay put," Phoebe said. "You told me not to leave Kyle's place until you got there. That's how Jimmy Johnston knew where you were going, right?"

Levesque nodded. His face was sour. "Cell phones," he said. "You end up having conversations in places that aren't necessarily private."

"Jimmy started to get worried," Steve said. "Caleb knew his grandfather had been wearing that vest when he was shot. He'd been waiting nine years to talk to Jimmy and try to get him to tell the truth about what had happened to Matthew Sunday. Then the chief came along and kept asking questions. Jimmy was afraid that maybe Caleb had told the chief about the vest — and that the chief believed him. And Jimmy was the only person who knew that the vest was missing and that no one had ever found it. Maybe that was making him nervous, too."

Levesque grimaced as he shifted against his pillows. "Shooting me would kill two birds with one stone," he said. "It would stop me from asking too many questions and maybe finding out what really happened to Matthew Sunday. And it would point the blame at Caleb and get him out of the way."

Mom shuddered and squeezed his hand. "Can you prove it?" she asked.

"Well, we have a statement from Freddy Deneuve that Jimmy drove away from the camp right after the chief," Steve said. "And we found tire impressions from Jimmy's van off the road north of the Darkes' place, so we know he was in the area recently. And it was one of his weapons that was involved in the shooting." He shrugged. "Jimmy's got so many charges against him now that the Crown will probably be able to make some kind of deal. I think he's looking at some time away from here."

Good, I thought.

* * *

Ross was waiting at the entrance to the hospital when Phoebe and Kyle and I walked out. He came toward us. "How is he?" he asked me.

"Mom says he'll be home by the end of the week. But he won't be going back to work for a while."

Ross nodded and looked at Kyle.

I nudged him. He actually looked scared. I nudged him again.

"Kyle?" he said.

Kyle looked at him.

"Can I talk to you for a minute?" Ross said.

Kyle nodded, and he and Ross went outside. I watched them through the glass. Ross was doing all the talking. Kyle was nodding.

"What's that all about?" Phoebe said.

I just shrugged. "Maybe you're not the only friend Kyle has any more," I said.

Phoebe looked at the two of them and smiled.

* * *

A week later, Phoebe and I were hurrying home from school. We had stopped at the grocery store on the way. Mom had gone up to Morrisville that afternoon to pick up Levesque; we were going to make a welcome-home supper. As we raced by the United Church with our bags of groceries, Phoebe said, "Look."

I turned.

Terri Tyson was sitting in her wheelchair beside the daycare playground. She was watching the little kids playing. Sitting on a bench on one side of her was Caleb. He was holding her hand. Kyle sat at her other side. He was talking — maybe to Terri, maybe to Caleb, maybe to both of them.

I think that was the first time I had ever seen him look content.